FLETCHER

Fire Lake – Book 2

M. Tasia

ALSO BY M. TASIA

The Boys of Brighton series
Gabe

Sam's Soldiers

Rick's Bear

Jesse

Coop

Travis

Grady

Vincent

Shadow

The Holidays

The Gates of Heaven series
Saint

Finn

James

Joey

Bradley

Carlos

Sawyer

Trey

Fire Lake series
Brick

EVERYONE LOVES THE BOYS OF BRIGHTON

"I loved this book and I love this town. I hope there's going to be more."
—Melissa Lemons on *Gabe*

"An amazing read that was filled with lust, love, crazy hot sex, danger, action and so much more This is the first book I have read in this series but I will definitely be reading more in the future."
—Gay Book Reviews on *Sam's Soldiers*

"I was crazy impressed that the author made me teary over the ending of a relationship that I shouldn't have even been invested in. I didn't yet know these characters yet the author made me hurt for them. That takes some mad writing skills!"
—Love Bytes Reviews

"Jesse and Royce together have my heart. Jesse has it all by himself."
—The Book Junkie Reads on *Jesse*

"So much action, intrigue, drama and angst for the long awaited story of Grady and Ben. This was worth the wait. Sexy and sweet. I can't wait for the next."
—SamD on *Grady*

"I knew this one would be my favorite to date! There was something about Vincent that said awesome then came Tristan."
—Booky on *Vincent*

"This installment of the Boys of Brighton was so good! I loved Shadow and Randy 's story I was hooked from the first page to the last. This book was definitely worth the wait!"
—AG on *Shadow*

"I have loved this series from the very first story and this holiday novella is simply perfect. We get a glimpse of all our couples and what is happening in their lives while the holidays explode around them. I cannot wait for more!"

—bookobsessed on *The Holidays*

ANOTHER BIG LOVE – THE GATES

"Ms. Tasia has done it again! This is Saint's story, for readers of the Brighton Boys, you'll know he needs a break! After being forced to become a plastic surgeon by his father, he rebels by assisting people in 3rd world countries, which puts him in the position to be kidnapped and tortured. You really feel for him, that's for sure! Max is the perfect man for poor Saint's battered soul, not that he doesn't have his own issues! Overall, this was engaging, steady paced and chock full of all the feels!"
—Avid Reader on *Saint*

"Finn and Miguel stole my heart. This is a great Sunday afternoon read. Finn's character jumped off the page as his story developed through each chapter. I loved reading his truth and watching him and Miguel find their home in each other."
—K.A. Brown on *Finn*

"This is really a great series and I def recommend it. I loved James and Ross, it was a rough start for the two, but they worked it out. I can't wait for more, love everything M. TASIA writes!"
—TammyKay on *James*

"I may have my new favorite book couple of the series. Joey and Sam just have that something special. At one point I was ugly crying but it was a good ugly cry if that makes any sense. I really love the series and I can't wait for her next installment!!"
—Vine Voice on *Joey*

"This author is really talented and I love her series, this one and the Boys of Brighton. Her characters are so well drawn and I can really get into the stories. I especially loved Eric in this particular book. I'm hoping Clay the rookie will be the next book. Keep 'em coming!"
—Rosemary on *Bradley*

"Two men with damaged souls come together and find love. A tried and true formula that works well here, especially when working with two lovable characters like Carlos and Clay. Carlos especially was interesting to me - the contrast of his appearance to his gentle nature, a true gentle giant. And Clay being all protective of the much larger, but more gentle man - so sweet! I really liked this story and am looking forward to more of The Gates now."
—Valeen on *Carlos*

"Sawyer is the newest addition to The Gates series. The book is very emotional, sweet, funny, romantic, and these two are great together. I look forward to every book in this series."
—Elaine Gray on *Sawyer*

"This book has all the feels and pulls the reader right in. It was wonderful to see how the two of them went from adversaries to respect to falling in love. You won't want to miss their story to see the path they travel and if there is a HEA waiting at the end. There is much more going on here, but hopefully this is enough to convince you that you will not want to miss this one."
~Emily Pennington on *Trey*

READERS ARE WILD ABOUT FIRE LAKE

"What a great beginning to a series! Brick and Roman are perfect together. Add in the murder factor and some well trained military men and you have the makings of an awesome series. It was a well written story that kept me engaged from the first page. Cannot wait for Fletch, Spencer, and Shaw's book."
~I Love Books 2005

www.BOROUGHSPUBLISHINGGROUP.com

FLETCHER
Copyright © 2021 M. Tasia

ISBN: 978-1-953810-89-2

To my family for their unwavering support.
I love all of you to the moon and back.

ACKNOWLEDGMENTS

To all my readers: Thank you. There's no escaping the truth – without all of you, there wouldn't be me, the author. Your support and kind words has taken me from being a new author who was unsure and panicked to an author with over twenty books under her belt. Okay, I'm still unsure and panicked, but I'm a work in progress. (Takes a sip of wine.)

I love sharing my stories with you and hearing how my characters have touched you and how you've cheered them on, cried with them, and even wanted to knock some sense into a few. Your encouragement has inspired me to continue on my writing journey. All the late nights, missed events, and looming deadlines have been worth it knowing these stories have entertained and stayed with you long after the book is finished.

FLETCHER

Chapter One

The jarring of mortar rounds exploding around him battered the earth, sending sand and rocks to rain down on Fletcher's body. He didn't move. He wouldn't move. Every "whomp" of their muzzle-loading grenade launcher announced another volley of shells being shot into the air from two hundred yards away.

Their exact position had yet to be discovered, but the enemy was getting closer with every shot. Self-preservation urged him to run. Thousands of man-hours of training made him stay. The enemy was fishing with dynamite. Unsure who or what was out there but willing to blow up everything to find out.

Every exploding shell increased the probability that sooner or later one would strike its mark. He had ten battle brothers alongside him hunkered down on these rocky hills while they waited for air support to hit the enemy target. The team had the place painted with laser sights, making it clearer for the incoming missiles to hit their marks.

If they moved now, the mission would be a bust and the enemy base below would continue supplying bombs to terrorists. Same storyline, different locations and faces changed over the years. Every time they brought down one asshole another rose from the ashes to take his place.

That's why there'd always be a call for men and women like him to hold the line out in the middle of nowhere. No fancy parades, only the plane ride would welcome them home as they would remain nameless along with the places they fought.

"Five klicks," someone said through his earpiece. Fighter jets were five kilometers out and closing fast. Another deluge of shells from the enemy rained down east of their location, causing searing pain to shoot through his left side. Fletch groaned, but he remained glued to his spot.

"Report," Brick whispered from his position high on the hill.

"Scratch, sir." *Bullshit.* He wouldn't tell them he'd been hit. His team was depending on him.

Before their leader could say more, another teammate's voice broke the silence. "We have squirters heading out the east gate."

Fletch looked over, and sure enough several vehicles were racing out of the compound into the dark desert heading in the opposite direction of the incoming jets. They must've had radar in the facility warning them an airstrike was imminent. The hum of truck engines didn't drown out the fighter jet engines approaching from the west.

He and the rest of his teammates stood their ground, ensuring every vital section of the factory was laser marked for destruction. They weren't concerned about barracks or small outbuildings. They wanted the machines the terrorists used to create bombs to be decimated after they left.

His side was burning like a fire poker was being jammed into him, but he didn't move.

They'd been staking out this plot of sand for more than twelve days, and when the missiles found their marks and the plumes of fire rose high into the night sky, it felt almost cathartic. Their mission was complete and a success. Fletch didn't give himself long to admire their hard work, instead he rolled onto his back to take a closer look at the damage he sustained from the last mortar round.

His side was saturated in blood. Never a good sign. He held the torn edges of his damaged shirt in either hand before ripping it open to find a piece of steel poking out from between his ribs. "Shit."

"Call in a bird. We need a dust-off," Brick ordered from Fletch's side. Fletch hadn't heard him coming, which said something about his pain level. He knew Brick moved fast, but damn, it was like he'd flown over here.

"I don't need to be medevacked," Fletch groaned. "It's probably not deep." Though the rush of blood was becoming concerning and suggested otherwise, he wouldn't show weakness.

Fletch pressed the fistful of gauze Brick handed him against his torn flesh made that way by the metal protruding from his side while his other brothers stood guard in case the assholes doubled back. As quickly as Brick was unwrapping the med dressings, they became saturated with blood. This wasn't looking good.

He stared at the stars overhead. They were more beautiful and brighter out here in the middle of the dunes. His head was pounding and his movements began to slow to the point where Brick took over applying pressure to his wound while Shaw pulled out more medical supplies. Fletch could hear Spence in the background yelling into his headset for a helicopter.

"Fletch, stay awake," Brick ordered.

He hadn't realized he was falling asleep, but the harder he worked to stay awake, the deeper he sank until all he could concentrate on were his stained hands covered in his own blood. He was bleeding out for his country in a war to stop bloodshed raining down on innocent civilians. What was his life compared to the many people who would be safe now that the bombs and the materials to make them were destroyed?

"Don't you die on me, you redheaded bastard," Brick ordered.

Fletch was too tired to listen as the world became darker around him, if that was even possible. The stars blinked in and out, or it might've been his eyelids struggling to stay open.

Damn, his parents had been right. He was going to die in some no-name patch of earth, saving people who would never know his name. Jerks. He wondered if dear old dad would find it a fitting ending for all the disappointment he'd caused the man.

He heard his heartbeat slow, and his brothers' voices were fading. He realized he'd begun gasping. He couldn't get enough air to fill his lungs.

This was it. His swan song.

At least he was surrounded by his family of battle brothers and sisters.

They would remember him.

***

Fletch jackknifed up in his bed as the piercing screech of his old alarm clock demanded his attention. His heart was pounding, and he looked down at his hands to find they were clean, not a hint of blood. Fumbling, he pulled up his t-shirt and ran his fingers over the long-healed scar winding from his hip bone to his lower rib cage. A constant reminder of how close to death he'd gotten and how fortunate he was to have a second chance.

"Turn that shit off," Spence yelled from the other side of Fletch's bedroom door. He gave the wood a few extra pounds with his fist for good measure. "Who the hell sets an alarm that loud anyway? Wake the damn dead." His voice was fading. No doubt, Spence was walking toward the kitchen and coffee.

Fletch reached over and hit the off button, giving silence its reign once more. He released a long slow breath before falling back against the mattress to stare at the cracked ceiling. They had to get around to replacing the drywall in the house someday soon.

Now that the roof was watertight, there was no need to fear future leaks. His eyes followed a particularly long crack from the window up the wall across the ceiling and back down until it disappeared into the doorjamb.

Fletch raked the palm of his hand down his sweat-covered face. It'd been months since the nightmare of nearly dying had hit him that hard. He couldn't help but wonder why it would return now. It had taken him over half a year to be considered fit to return to his SEAL team. Worst six months he'd ever had while in the service.

He'd been forced to watch his team prepare for missions without him, and was left behind to wait for word on their fate. The entire time he knew his absence could be responsible for the death of any of his team. It sucked, and he refused to be put into that position again.

Now he knew how military families felt every time their loved ones left for duty. That was why it was best not to have attachments outside his team. They were his friends and brothers. Besides, he'd tried and it never stuck.

With a loud huff, Fletch pushed himself off the bed and grabbed his workout clothes. He could put in a couple of hours before the rest of the team was up. Other than Spence, who was downstairs banging around in the kitchen thanks to Fletch's alarm clock. He'd have to get a new one, or Spence would find a way to make him pay. Considering he was their information specialist, payback could come in any form. Hell, he could wake up to having his identity wiped out of existence. *Hmm, that might not be so bad.*

After he used the bathroom and changed, he headed out of his room, turned left down the old staircase and out the garden doors before Spence had a chance to spit out a word. Sure, he'd have to deal with him sooner or later, but right now later sounded like the best option. Let Spence get some coffee in him first.

Fletch stretched his arms over his head as he walked toward the dirt road behind the lake house. On either side of the house sat thick brush and copses of trees enclosing his former team leader's land.

Fletch decided to start with a five-mile run before working out with weights, and then going a few rounds with the heavy bag they'd installed in a quasi-gym of sorts beside the shed. The "gym" had a roof on ten-foot posts, but its walls were open to let the breeze flow through. Helped on those especially hot days.

He shook out his legs and began with a slow jog in the direction of the main road. Typically, he'd run down to the end of the peninsula to piss off Roman's asshole father, but he didn't feel the urge today. Brick and his man Roman were working on their relationship with the elder Furrow, but for Fletch nothing could excuse what he'd tried to do to make Julia get Brick to sell his house.

Who threatens to fire someone if they didn't prostitute themselves out to get the sale? A rich asshole who thinks he has the right to use people to get what he wants. That's who. At least Julia was working for them now, and she and her son were safe. Fletch would make sure it stayed that way.

As far as Fletch was concerned, Stephan Furrow was a complete bastard. Shaking his head to clear his thoughts, Fletch increased his pace as if he wasn't working hard enough. *Suck it up, Seaman.*

Stretching out his legs, he began eating up the road. With every flex of his muscles, he felt the burn driving him forward. His arms pumped as he gained control over his breathing until only the sound of his running shoes pounding against the pavement gave him away.

The morning mist hovering mere feet above the ground floated among the lotebushes and other thorn brush growing by the side of the road. It wouldn't take long for the mist to burn off with the emerging sun. He heard the birds sing as they took to the sky. He loved this time of day. Anything was possible in the early morning light. Everything had been washed clean the night before and the world could start anew with the sun. It felt like a symphony of rebirth and hope, though he'd never admit these flowery thoughts to the guys. They'd give him quantum shit if he got all poetic. Besides, he wasn't much of a talker.

Not one vehicle had driven past him, and he'd been running for over thirty minutes. To say the lake house was off the beaten path was an understatement. It took close to an hour to drive to Marshall, the closest town, which had the basics: a grocery store, bar, diner, post office, sheriff's substation, fire station, gas station, hair salon, a few retail stores, two traffic lights, four stop signs, and a school with an impressive football field. Typical small Texas town.

An alarm sounded on his watch alerting him to the halfway mark of his run. He made a big loop and headed back toward Sophia's place. Sophia was the original owner, who left the lake house to Brick, her great-nephew. The team had been working on renovating it within months of Brick moving in. Between cases and crappy weather. He'd spent more time in the root cellar than he'd like to admit to.

The cases were from LH Investigations, a private security and investigation agency he and his former teammates ran and worked. After leaving the SEALs, they'd formed a new unit. No longer active military, the four new business owners had already solved five cases in the few months since they'd signed LH Investigations into existence.

Fletch had never imagined he'd be a co-owner of anything. His family would be shocked a grunt like him made good instead of being some *dumb target*, which was what they'd referred to him as in his chosen career. The SEALs and service to his country weren't high on their list of good jobs.

Hell, when he'd signed up for the Navy, the only one who came to say good-bye was his younger brother. The rest of the family had written him off, convinced he'd be killed in the line of duty.

Harsh, but for his family, not shocking. Out of the six of them, five were geniuses. He was not. His parents were professors, his two older sisters worked the research and development for a pharmaceutical giant, and his younger brother, Kyle, recently sold his first start-up for over thirty-three million dollars. Fletch had barely made it through high school. Had it not been for his ability to play football well, the coach wouldn't've been able to get him the extra help he needed to graduate.

His parents and sisters were disgusted he'd received a scholarship to a prestigious university to play a "stupid game." To them, he was a fraud, and all his achievements during college were written off as fake no matter how much tutoring he received and how hard he tried. He was no Einstein, but those college grades were his own. He'd earned them through late nights of studying, staying behind after class to ask questions, and having a study group where his fellow students tutored him.

Fletch had done everything in his power to make his family proud, but nothing worked. On graduation day, when he walked across the stage to collect his diploma, he looked out to the audience to find only his brother in attendance sitting beside four empty seats Fletch had reserved for the rest of his family.

The next day he'd signed up with the Navy. If his hard-fought-for mediocre grades didn't work, serving his country surely would. He was so naïve back then. However, what was yet another failed attempt to make his parents proud had turned into him finding the family he never had.

His battle brothers and sisters never failed him, and secure in that knowledge, he was where he belonged. He'd found his place in the world. He knew the parameters and what was expected of him. Hard work earned praise and promotions with no strings attached. He understood and embraced the culture instead of the continual guessing of what would make his family happy.

He and Kyle were still close. As for the rest of the family, they were estranged. Fletch didn't return home when he had time off between missions. There was no reason to go back to them. Kyle would fly to San Diego and visit with him on Coronado Island where the SEALs were based.

For the life of him, Fletch had no idea why his family was front and center in his mind this morning or why his nightmares had returned. It might have something to do with getting settled in a new place and all the changes going on around him. Going from a Navy SEAL to a business owner was a leap Fletch was still trying to get accustomed to.

Twenty years' worth of missions across the globe had given him perspective on his family situation. He understood there wouldn't be a way to make his parents and sisters change their minds no matter what he did. So he stopped caring...mostly. Their estrangement still stung at times.

He shook his head again, causing his hair to stick to the side of his sweaty face and neck. Usually, he tied his hair back, but he'd left in such a hurry this morning he'd left his hair band on his dresser. Without breaking stride, he pulled his t-shirt over his head and used it to wipe the sweat from his face and neck before balling it up in one hand for the rest of his run.

The breeze felt refreshing against his heated skin. The wide-open, blue sky laid out before him as if anything were possible. After several more minutes, he heard the first vehicle coming down the road behind him. He made sure to move over onto the shoulder until the vehicle passed. But it didn't pass. In fact, it began to slow.

With a quick glance back, Fletch knew his day was taking a definite turn as the sheriff's cruiser slowed until it traveled at the same pace at his side.

"Sheriff. What'd I do to deserve your attention this morning?" Fletch asked the handsome lawman who'd starred in many of Fletch's happier dreams. "Or couldn't you stay away?"

Chapter Two

Elias knew this was a mistake, but it didn't stop him from slowing down. He liked to drive in different areas of his county in the early morning before most people were awake. The radio was silent, and he had his windows rolled down, allowing the not-for-long cool air to rush through the cab of his vehicle. It was serene and as peaceful as his life got. He treasured it.

He hadn't had much time off after retiring from the Marines and becoming the sheriff of Marshall County. Four thousand, two hundred and sixty-eight square miles of land with a population of slightly over one hundred and fifty thousand residents spread far and wide. Elias never regretted his decision to take the position, but some days were harder than others.

If he'd gotten a job in a more urban area, he'd have a much better chance of blending in. However, in a county full of fields and ranchers, a six-foot-five gay black man stood out. His dating life had dried up, and he'd been considering taking a drive into Austin to hit a few clubs. People in the county were friendly enough, but he'd have to look elsewhere if he wanted to find someone to date.

At least that was until a group of former SEALs moved into Sophia's old lake house and began fixing it up. One redhead kept coming to mind no matter how hard Elias tried to ignore the guy. Elias was a grown-ass man nursing a teenage crush. As if mentioning him brought Fletcher Daniels to life, he appeared ahead jogging on the side of the road.

Without conscious thought, Elias's foot eased off the gas pedal and his cruiser began to slow. It would be rude to drive by without checking in. He could ask about LH Investigations, the former SEALs' new business. *Yeah, that's plausible.*

He was so screwed.

Elias nearly swallowed his tongue as he got a closer look as Fletch's muscles flexed and bunched along his back and down to his glutes. His arms and legs pumped in unison, eating up the distance and surprising Elias when he looked down at his speedometer. Fletch was fast, and Elias appreciated a man who worked hard to stay in shape, as he did.

"Sheriff. What'd I do to deserve your attention this morning?" Fletch asked. "Or couldn't you stay away?"

"Out on patrol," Elias answered. "Wouldn't be neighborly if I drove by without slowing to say hello."

"Ahh, is that what this is?" Fletch laughed. "Friendly sheriff watching over his flock."

"Yeah, something like that," he replied, unable to keep the grin off his face. "How's the new business going?"

Fletch slowed to an easy jog and used his balled-up shirt to wipe the sweat off his face and broad chest. Something Elias would like to do and often, especially after "working out" with Fletch. "Honestly, it's going better than I thought it would."

"Good news. Have any interesting cases?" Engaging Fletch in conversation would give Elias more time with the handsome man, but he truly was interested in how the team was coming along in their new venture.

The object of his desire slowed even further until he came to a stop and turned to face Elias, who brought his cruiser to a stop and threw it into park.

"We've had the usual cheating husbands who weren't worried enough to try to cover their tracks. A case of fraud where a woman assumed the identity of her dead sister, and a stakeout to gather enough proof to break up a ring of car thieves working the east end of San Antonio."

"Huh. Interesting," Elias said. "You enjoy it?"

Fletcher looked tired. Agitated. "Yeah," he said, but his expression told a different story. Something was bugging the guy. He looked stressed out.

"Then why do you look so unhappy?" Cooper asked as he got out of the car and stood leaning his back against his cruiser.

"Got some old memories I'm trying to rebury," was Fletch's vague response. "It has nothing to do with the business."

"Anything I can do to help?" Elias couldn't stop the offer from leaving his mouth. It seemed he was in deep when it came to his red-headed SEAL.

"Nah. Unfortunately, you can't choose my biological family."

"Don't I know it. My uncle's in McConnell State Prison outside Beeville serving a life sentence. Family reunions are always fun." Half his family didn't have much use for the law.

"Prison is likely where most of my family assumed I was heading," Fletch admitted with a shake of his head. "They never had faith in me."

"Get into trouble when you were younger?" Elias asked.

"No, more like the least intelligent person in a family full of IQs over one thirty."

Elias could feel his anger rising. "Let me get this straight. They assumed you'd be a criminal because of some test you took?"

"It's more complicated than that and better left in the past," Fletch said before redirecting the conversation. "How're things in the area? Any great mysteries needing solving in Marshall?"

Elias dropped the subject and couldn't help but laugh at the knowing smirk on Fletch's face. "I'm afraid nothing to rival your car thieves. Big news. Mr. Ager's cattle broke out of their pasture again, making it the third time in the last two weeks. He's still missing three Angus steers."

"Cattle rustling, eh?" Fletch had his cowboy drawl down pat.

"More like cattle wandering. If you or any of your team see them, let me know so we can round 'em up and get 'em back to where they belong."

"I can do that. I'll let the guys and Julia know to keep an eye out," Fletch offered, always ready to lend a hand.

"Much obliged," Cooper said while tipping his hat. "It's good to know you townsfolk can be called upon when the need arises." He had no idea why he was behaving like some old-time western movie sheriff, but Fletch seemed to like it.

"Well, golly. That's mighty kind of you." Fletch laughed before stretching out his legs.

"I'll let you get back to your run," Elias said while opening his car door.

"Yeah, I should finish my workout," Fletch replied, and for a moment Elias thought Fletch looked disappointed.

Elias sat behind the steering wheel and shut the door. "I'll be seeing you around, Fletch."

"Cooper," Fletch said with a nod of his head. Then he turned around and broke into a run, heading in the direction of the lake house.

Elias took a few moments to watch him go before putting the cruiser into drive and heading back to Marshall and his office. He had four deputies working out of his division and had yet to post next month's shift schedule. If he didn't get it done soon, he'd be hearing about it.

Forty minutes later he was pulling into the substation's parking lot in time to see one of his deputies haul off and punch another deputy in the gut. *What the hell?* Elias pulled up behind their cruisers then jumped out to get some answers.

"Harris and Sanchez. What's going on here?" His voice echoed against the brick wall of the substation.

"Harris asked me to hit him, sir," Sanchez said with his hands up, palms out on either side of his head.

Elias shook his head. "Why the hell would you do that?"

"I've been working on my core strength and wanted to see if I could take a hit," Harris answered, a healthy dose of regret in his tone.

"And what'd you discover?" Shit. Elias was surrounded by children.

"I need to work on it some more," Harris replied while rubbing his stomach.

"Do me a favor; the next time you want someone to punch you, wait until you're inside the damn building. That way the public won't have to watch two idiots who get paid by those taxpayers who are supposed to protect them. Not be out here hauling off on one another. Got it?"

"Yes, sir."

"Yes, Sheriff."

"Better yet? How 'bout not doing it at all, hmmm?"

They nodded and looked sheepish.

"Good. Now let's get this day started," Elias ordered while pointing at the door leading into the station. "Gentlemen, if you please." He followed his deputies inside, stopping by reception and dispatch to check if any new messages or alerts were waiting for him.

"Morning, Marie," he said as he took a file from his inbox. "Anything pressing?" Marie had been with the sheriff's office for going on thirty years next month. They were planning a party over at Clancy's bar.

"Morning, Sheriff. Ms. James over on Tenant Road reported seeing a couple head of cattle out near Fraser Point. Jeff Walton and Molly came by looking to talk to you. He said you could find him down at the marina. And the coyote that's been hanging around the dump is getting closer to people now."

"Lost its fear of humans. We'll have to get a trapper out there to relocate the coyote far away from civilization." He wouldn't kill it if he didn't have to.

"I'll give old Jerome a call. He and his son should be up for the job," Marie offered.

"Thanks. I'll stop by and check in with Jeff after roll call."

Elias shoved the file under his arm and headed to the conference room where Harris, Sanchez, Reynolds, and Bryant sat waiting for him. The team already knew their assignments for the day, but this was their chance to catch up on the county's happenings.

"Morning, everyone. I trust you've all been made aware of what is considered appropriate behavior outside these walls?" he asked.

"Yes, sir," Reynolds said.

"Idiots." Bryant laughed as she stared over at the two deputies who'd behaved like idiots, but Elias couldn't say that out loud. "Next time, ask me to punch you, Harris. I won't hold back."

"Hey, I didn't hold back," Sanchez shot back while rubbing his knuckles.

All four laughed, making Elias grin. "Okay, okay. Let's bring this meeting to order. Reynolds, I need you to go up to Fraser Point, got a report of some cattle wandering loose."

"Are they Mr. Agre's missing steers that got out the other day?" Reynolds asked.

"We'll know when you get your eyes on them. Keep me updated. Sanchez, that coyote over on dump road is becoming a dangerous nuisance. We put a call out to Jerome and his son to see if they can trap and relocate it."

"Got it. I'll watch out for them."

"Harris and Bryant, you have your assignments, and there's nothing new to report in those areas. Now let's discuss something more pleasing, Marie's party."

"Everything is set up with Clancy over at the bar," Sanchez said.

"Mrs. Williams will be taking care of the cake over at the diner," Reynolds added.

"Gifts have been purchased," Bryant said. "But someone else is going to have to wrap them. I can't wrap worth a damn."

"You can't wrap?" Harris teased as he put his feet up on the desk.

"Feet down, Harris."

"Sorry, Sheriff."

"What? Do you think all women instinctively know how to wrap perfectly? Pick out the right bow? Maybe add some damn glitter?" Bryant cringed with every word as if she were describing some horrible torture.

"No. It's because you're so perfect at everything," Harris teased while batting his eyes at her.

"Jealous?" She grinned.

"Me, never."

"Yeah, right. The last time you two faced off in competition, blood was shed," Sanchez reminded everyone. "Not a good idea."

"It wasn't mine," Bryant said before smiling wide.

"I needed stitches." Harris pouted.

"You needed a bandage."

"Okay, you two. I'll wrap the damn presents," Elias stated, having enough of their adolescent banter. They could go on like that for hours.

"Can we bring a date?" Harris asked.

"Seriously, is every event a chance for you to hook up?" Bryant huffed.

"No, but it helps," Harris replied.

"And on that note, get out." Elias shook his head and pointed at the door. "You have jobs to do. Be safe out there."

His four deputies stood to leave, still talking about Harris's dating life. His team had been together for over five years, and he wouldn't change a damn thing about any of them even when they drove him nuts when they behaved like children. Which was often.

He walked to his office, threw his Stetson on the coat rack, and sat behind his desk. He opened the file he'd had tucked under his arm and threw it down onto the worn wood surface. Not even a quarter of the way through reading the report, his mind wandered back to earlier that morning.

What would Fletch say if he asked him out on a date, or to Marie's party? Would Elias's position as sheriff put an end to anything before it began? It was only one of the possibilities among many for them getting together to turn out badly. Hell, maybe Harris was rubbing off on him.

Damnit, you're a Marine. Act like one.

This infatuation was going to end badly. No doubt about it.

Elias dropped the file and stood. "Marie, I'm going down to the marina to speak with Jeff."

The paperwork could wait for when he was less distracted.

Whenever the hell that might be.

Chapter Three

"Where the hell is my hammer?" Brick yelled down from the top of a twenty-foot ladder.

"Language, Uncle Brick," Julia yelled back.

Fletch bent over and picked up a hammer from the ground. "Is this it?"

"Sorry, and yeah, that's the one."

"You must've left it down here, man."

"Got that," Brick huffed.

"Don't worry. I'll bring it up with the birdhouse."

Brick had cleared a spot on a sizeable tree for Sammy's birdhouse. After over a week of construction with Sammy, Julia's five-year-old son, as the team lead, they'd finished painting the exterior yesterday. It had a front porch, tiny shutters, a chimney, and all the fresh nesting material birds could want. These birds never had it so good.

Fletch picked up the red and white birdhouse and settled it onto his shoulder before sliding the hammer onto his tool belt. On a separate ladder, he made his way up to Brick in no time as Sammy and Julia watched from a safe distance on the deck around the fire pit. The landscaping had come a long way from overgrown weeds to an actual lawn.

"Let me help," Brick said as Fletch felt the weight lifted from his shoulder.

He took the opportunity to grab the hammer from his belt and hand it to Brick. "Here you go."

"Thanks, man. Can't keep my head on straight today," Brick grumbled.

"I'm sure when Roman gets in from Dallas tonight, you'll be back to your normal pain in the ass self," Fletch joked. "I know he's been away for over a week, and I'm surprised you haven't left for the city by now." Fletch didn't understand all Brick's pining. He thought the whole *I need you near me* angst was bullshit.

"Joke all you want, but when it happens to you, you'll get it," Brick taunted with a grin before hammering the rest of the boards onto the tree.

"Yeah, well, with my track record, that won't be happening any time soon." To say his love life was a little dry would be like saying a sandstorm was a light breeze. He pushed the birdhouse up higher so Brick could position it on the side of the over one hundred-year-old tree with its thick trunk. The heavy lug nuts would ensure their new tenants would be safe and secure in a windstorm.

"What about your sheriff?" Brick asked.

"He's not 'my' anything. Hell, we barely have conversations." He couldn't help but think back to the other morning when he was out for his run. It'd been the perfect opportunity to ask the guy out. But again: nothing.

"That's because it's always in passing," Brick stated. "You gotta pin the man down and talk. Get to know him."

"I haven't worked up to that yet." *Pathetic.*

"You met him months ago. How long's this 'working up' gonna take? Ask him out to coffee at the diner," Brick suggested. "Or have him come here. Julia's got that fancy coffee machine." He wagged his brows. "It'll make an impression."

"You make that shit sound easy, but it's not that simple." It never was.

"When's the last time you went out on a date?"

Fletch knew when. It might as well have been tattooed across his chest. He could never forget his last real date. "That time before that West African mission to free the kidnapped news crew."

He held the birdhouse in place as Brick bolted it down. Nice addition to the lake house. Made it feel homier instead of being only a frat house full of guys. Glancing down, he saw Sammy bouncing on his toes while holding on to his mom's hand. His blond hair looked nearly invisible in the bright sunlight, and his smile was wide.

The whole team was attached to the kid. They would've made him a bird condo if the little guy wanted one. Sammy was everyone's buddy, and he followed the team around like a puppy. Julia was an exceptional mom, but she was forever reprimanding them about their language and reminding them to watch what stories they told in front of her son.

"That should do it," Brick said. "Let her go."

Fletch took a step down on his ladder and allowed all the weight to rest on the bolts. It didn't budge.

"Look, man," Brick said from his place at the top of the other ladder, "I'm always around to talk. I know you liked Alaine and were disappointed when things went south."

"Roman's making you soft," Fletch stated. "What happened to the man who could barely make it through team member yearly reviews? You despised talking."

"You learn and evolve to life's changes." Brick nodded as if that explained it all.

Alaine and Fletch had been dating for months when he got word the team was headed to Africa. He'd expected Alaine to be worried, not to get the *it's not you, it's me* speech after he explained in way too much detail how he wasn't cut out to be a military spouse waiting to hear whether Fletch made it out alive. And who knew for how long Alaine would have to be alone.

Fletch couldn't figure out why Alaine started a relationship with him. If it was just to have the Navy SEAL notch on his fuck belt, they could've had a night or two, not months.

Alaine was the last in a long line of men who got off on sleeping with Fletch because of what he did. None of them had any intention of sticking around for the long haul. He hadn't believed Alaine fit in that category and "disappointed" didn't cover how Alaine's good-bye affected him. Fletch had no intention of going down that road again. He'd lived with too much alienation from the people who were supposed to love him. He didn't have it in him to court more of the same.

Empty fucks were his future. He wasn't wallowing in self-pity. This was the best outcome. He knew what he was getting, what to expect, and only the lower half of his body was involved, and that involvement was brief.

"Uncle Fletch, Uncle Brick," Sammy yelled as they got to the bottom of their ladders. "It looks great." Then he ran straight at Fletch.

"Thanks, kid." Fletch lifted the small dude into the air, making him squeal.

"It came out nice," Julia said as she joined them. "Thank you for taking the time to build the birdhouse with him."

"You don't need to thank us," Brick said.

"Yeah, we're family," Fletch chimed in. "You do stuff for family." At least with these people, his chosen family.

He raised Sammy high into the air to play his favorite game, airplane. Sammy stretched his arms and legs wide and began making adorable engine noises.

"Base to team leader, come in, Sammy." Brick cupped his hands and lowered his voice, playing along. Brick and Roman would make great parents.

"I'm here," Sammy giggled in response.

"Time to land and have lunch, buddy."

"Do I have to?" Sammy whined while flapping his arms.

Fletch lowered him into his arms. "You want to grow up big and strong like us, don't you?" He flexed his right bicep.

Sammy's eyes got big, and then he said, "I do. I'm hungry, Mom."

Fletch couldn't help but laugh. "I could eat," he agreed.

"Thank you guys for everything you've done for Sammy," Julia said before turning to lead the way into the house. "I can't think of better examples of how a good man is supposed to act than this team. I want him growing up knowing the difference."

"Thanks. Though I'm not positive we're the best examples." Brick laughed.

"Yeah, most of my family think I'm a failure," Fletch said. There weren't many secrets between their team members, and Fletch had talked about his brother before. He'd have to call Kyle soon and touch base, invite him out to the lake house for a visit.

Julia stopped to look up at him. "You are not a failure. You're a hero. Remember that. If they can't see that, you're better off without them." Julia was no more than five-two, but when she got riled up, stand back.

"Better off without who?" Spence asked from his spot on the porch where he was working on the wiring for their new exterior lighting.

"Fletch's family," Brick answered as Julia took Sammy from Fletch's arms and headed inside the house.

"Those assholes? Have they been bugging you?" Spence mumbled while looking at what he was doing.

"No, but they've been on my mind, and I can't seem to shake 'em." No matter how hard he tried.

"Is that why you've been up before the crack of dawn for over a week now?" Spence asked.

Fletch shrugged. His nightmares were his own to deal with.

"Why don't you invite Kyle down for a visit?" Brick suggested. "We have plenty of room."

"I was considering it. Maybe he can take a few days off. I'll try him." Fletch had to admit the idea made him feel lighter.

"Good idea," Spence said.

With a nod, Fletch pulled out his phone from his back pocket and walked down to the far end of the porch before hitting his brother's name. It rang once before his voice mail picked up. *You've reached Kyle Daniels. Please leave a message after the beep.* "Hey. Thought I'd give you a call to catch up and invite you out to the house on Fire Lake. It's the one I told you about a couple of months back that belongs to Brick. I decided to stick around. If you have a few days, it'd be great if you could come down. I could show you around. We've got a lot of work done, and started our own firm, LH Investigations. We're starting to pick up clients. Give me a call when you get this. Love you, bro."

***

Fletch had gone into Marshall to get food. The team had always eaten like each meal was their last, which in some cases it was until they wrapped up their mission. Rations sucked, and when they got back to base, they didn't eat, they sucked up food like vacuum cleaners. Doing all the house repairs had kicked up their appetites and they were going through munchies, veggies, and protein like sixteen-year-olds.

He loaded the last of the grocery bags and shut the tailgate on his new GMC Sierra 2500HD in Pacific blue metallic with a jet-black interior. He'd splurged and gotten the V8 Duramax Turbo-Diesel with ten-speed automatic transmission. This was the first new vehicle he'd ever bought for himself.

Spending all his adult life in the Navy without incurring any real expenses had netted him a sizeable nest egg when he retired. He had his normal pay, his danger pay, his re-up bonuses, and some extras. The only catch: he'd had to survive some of the most screwed-up, deadly situations a person could go through. The by-product? A lifetime of night terrors.

The rest of the team had convinced him to spend a little money on himself and even drove him to the dealership in San Antonio to make sure he got the exact model he'd wanted. He had to admit he was stoked. He'd bought this with his hard work. No free ride, as his parents so often stated. *Why can't I get them off my mind? Why hasn't my brother called me back?*

"Nice truck," a deep voice, which caused goosebumps to rise on his arms, said from behind him. "Is that this year's model?"

Fletch turned to see Sheriff Cooper stop a few feet away from him. The man was sex on a stick with his long legs, muscled arms and chest, cowboy boots, uniform, and Stetson. He had to have plenty of offers to play with his handcuffs.

"Yeah," Fletch said as he rubbed an imaginary speck of dust off the paint. "I picked her up a few days ago."

"Six-point-six liter?"

"V-eight."

"Nice. You can get a lot done in a truck like that."

Fletch's mind headed straight to what he wanted to do in his new truck and with whom. They could test out the truck bed. Imagining all the ways they could break in the truck caused his dick to press against the zipper of his jeans. Not comfortable.

Shit. I can't have a hard-on in front of the sheriff.

"Something wrong?" Intuitive bastard. Shit. Fletch hoped the sheriff couldn't see the bulge.

Fletch turned before he embarrassed himself completely and headed for the quad cab. The sheriff was hot on his heels, but Fletch managed to reach for the door handle and jumped into the driver's seat. "I'm good. Just had to sit down for a minute. I pulled a muscle during my morning run." *Yeah, that's plausible. He was having a hard time walking with the stiffy he was sporting.*

If the sheriff was suspicious, he didn't say anything. Instead, he leaned against the door and hit Fletch with a question he hadn't seen coming. "You know Marie, over at my office. Well, she's been working front desk dispatch for the past thirty years, and we're having a party for her over at Clancy's bar on Saturday night. I was wondering if you'd like to attend." He'd rushed through the last bit so fast Fletch wasn't sure he heard it all.

"Are you inviting me to go with you to the party?" A flash of excitement rushed through his body. His muscles tensed, and he could feel his heart speeding up. He liked the sheriff and getting to know him better would be good. Another friend. Someone else to hang out with. Maybe they'd—

"You and…um, the guys are welcome to celebrate with us. Stop by and have a beer with the townsfolk." The sheriff seemed to be struggling with his words.

Fletch's heart sank into his stomach. For a fraction of a second, he thought the handsome sheriff was asking him out when it was an invite for the entire team. It was the last nail in that coffin. He had to get over this infatuation with the sheriff. It was painfully obvious the man wasn't interested.

"Sure, I'll let the guys know." He couldn't help the slight growl in his voice, but quickly covered it with a cough.

"Okay, then. We'll see you guys on Saturday," the sheriff said as he stepped away from the truck.

Fletch knew a dismissal when he heard one. He pushed the ignition button, threw the truck into drive, and waved his good-bye. He had to get far away before he said something stupid. His hard-on had deflated as quickly as it'd started. It couldn't be more obvious that the man wasn't interested or was straight.

Fletch's instincts had never steered him so wrong before.

A hard lesson learned. "Leave the sheriff alone."

Chapter Four

What was wrong with him? Elias sat behind his desk stewing over what he'd said to Fletch about the party. He'd intended to invite Fletch as a date, but his brain misfired when the handsome guy asked one simple question.

"You know, you're working yourself into an ulcer," Marie said from his open doorway.

"I'm the sheriff. I'm contractually obligated to have ulcers," he joked, trying to dig his way out of the conversation Marie was building up to.

It didn't work. She came to sit in one of the chairs across the desk from him. "This has nothing to do with your profession. Ever since Sophia's great-nephew moved into town along with his friends, you've been anxious. Why is that?"

"I'm not worried about the team. They're ex-military and good people. Nothing to worry about there. They all check out." The last thing he wanted was for the people of Marshall to be suspicious of the new arrivals because their sheriff couldn't close the deal.

"That's not what I meant. Let's cut to the chase. The big guy with the red hair. Fletcher. He's got you wound up tighter than our mayor's purse strings." She sat back with her arms crossed over her chest. Damn it. He knew that move. She wasn't going anywhere.

As was her way, she went straight to the heart of the matter. He could respect that and shouldn't've been surprised. She'd seen a lot in her thirty years behind the reception desk and even before that as a high school math teacher. Nothing got by her.

She looked at him shrewdly. "Are you going to ask him out or continue wallowing for the foreseeable future?"

Elias never hid who he was, but he hadn't come outright and said "I'm gay" either. He didn't believe it was anyone's business and preferred it that way. But he didn't bother denying it either.

"The man is driving me insane and he doesn't even know it," he blurted out in frustration. "I can't even ask him out properly. Ask me to disarm a bomb, and I got it, but this? No."

"I wouldn't say he doesn't know you're attracted to him. His eyes light up every time he sees you," she said while giving him a withering look.

"They do?" He latched on to that piece of information like a lifeline.

"How old are you, son? Cause you're acting like a teenager with his first damn crush."

"Not to put too fine a point on it." *Ouch.* "But I don't want a—"

"Fuck?" she provided.

Okay then. "Yeah, that... With Fletcher."

Her face softened. "I haven't seen you date anyone since you took over the sheriff's position. If you're out of practice, I can offer my services."

"Offer your services?" That might be the scariest proposition he'd ever had.

"At my party, I can drop a few hints. Hell, I'm a cute old lady. Who'd suspect me? Let me tell you, there's plenty of stuff I get away with on the daily." She grinned.

"I don't want you dropping hints... Wait. How do you know about the party? It was supposed to be a surprise." Everyone in town knew not to tell her.

"Seriously, between me, Jeff, and the fishing crew, nothing gets by us in this county. Now, back to your problem."

"My problem?" He was having an out-of-the-body experience. Like looking down at the train wreck before it happened.

"Yes. Your inability to close the deal," she said matter-of-factly.

Was the woman in his head? "Close the deal?"

"Yep. Go out on a date. Do the horizontal tango. Make the moves on him. Whatever you young men call it these days." She waved her hand in the air.

"Okay, I want out of this conversation." He was not discussing his love life with a seventy-year-old lady, no matter how on the mark she was.

"Fine, have it your way, but the offer still stands if you need me." She stood and walked out the office door, then turned around to say, "But I wouldn't wait too long, or someone else might snap up the handsome man."

"Wait. What?"

"You're not the only one in town who has their eye on him," she said before closing the door behind her, ending any further questioning.

"Someone else?" The words soured in his mouth. "I don't fucking think so."

***

Fletch pulled up to Clancy's bar and parked his truck but didn't bother shutting the engine off.

"Here you go, guys," he said to his teammates. "Shoot me a text when you want to get picked up."

"Is this about the sheriff?" Roman asked from the backseat of Fletch's quad cab.

"Dude, you can't let him ruin the fun we could have tonight. I, for one, need a night off to sit back, drink a beer, and shoot the breeze with people who don't live at the lake house," Shaw said while trying to reach over Spence for the door handle. "My toned ass is going to be shaking it on the dance floor tonight."

"Your concern is noted," Fletch stated. "Now get out."

"You sure?" Brick asked. "You can come in and feel it out. We'll have a beer, say hello, congratulate Marie, and hit the road." Always the team leader.

"Yeah, man," Spence added. "We've got your back."

Fletch thought it over. It would be odd if he were the only one on the team not to show up. The bar was big enough for him and the sheriff. It could work. Besides, his plan to chew on his worry because Kyle hadn't called him back didn't sound particularly appealing.

"Okay, but swear you won't let me make a fool of myself in front of him." That's all he needed. Get drunk and come on to the guy who was not interested in him.

"You got it." Spence nodded.

"Definitely," Roman said.

"I've got you," Shaw weighed in. Fletch knew his friend might appear vain and self-centered, but you could depend on him to have your back.

"If that's what you want, we'll run interference," Brick said.

He had a feeling he was going to regret this, but he shut off the engine and got out anyway. Hell, he was a Navy SEAL and didn't do emotions. Emotions didn't rule him. At the end of the day, cold, hard logic ruled.

"Fuck the sheriff. Let's have some fun," Fletch growled as he and his friends rounded the corner of Clancy's bar, earning him a few slaps on the back.

There were plenty of trucks and a few cars in the gravel parking lot. A good turnout for the party. It'd give him the chance to meet some more locals, and who knows, he might even have fun. He stood straight and schooled his expression. He got this.

The full moon bathed the area in a grayish blue light, making for excellent visibility down the quiet main street. Marshall was a small town compared to most and far outside of what Fletch was used to, but surprisingly exactly what he needed at this time in his life. Peace and quiet.

Country music flowed over them as they opened the thick wooden doors to the bar, and Fletch couldn't help but go on alert as he took in the sea of people. Crowds could be difficult at times. Too much combat shit still stuffed in his head.

"Damn good turnout," Brick said as he wrapped his arm around Roman's back. "Let's get a drink."

Roman handed Fletch the card all of them had signed. They'd chipped in on a gift card. "Fletch. Find Marie and give this to her."

"Sure. I'll meet you back at the bar," Fletch said as he scanned the room for the woman of the hour. He'd met her once at the post office when he went to pick up the mail. She had almost white hair pinned up in a bun, was petite and round, and she wore a mischievous grin that told him more than any stats ever could. He liked her.

He followed the multicolored balloons over to the far side of the bar to a wall with half-moon booths. He saw Molly, Jeff's chocolate lab, lying on the floor beside one booth. Sure enough, Jeff, along with Tuck, Wreck, and Andy, the former military men, now fishing crew, were sitting in a booth along with Marie squished in at the center.

So far, so good. He hadn't seen the sheriff, but he doubted his luck would last. The handsome bastard stood taller than most men, so there'd be no missing him. Marie smiled wide as he neared the table.

"Good evening, ma'am," he said as he held out her card. "This is for you from the team. Congratulations on your thirty years with the sheriff's office." He nodded at the men seated with her.

She took the card and said, "Thank you, hon. This is so sweet of you boys."

"Would you like to join us?" Wreck asked.

"Thanks but I'm meeting up with the team at the bar." Fletch felt bad about refusing his offer, but if the sheriff were around, he'd come to this table. That would be the opposite of Fletch laying low.

A knowing expression crossed Marie's face as he scanned the room once again. "Let the boy have some fun. We'll catch up later."

"Yes, ma'am." Fletch silently thanked her for somehow understanding. With a quick good-bye, he turned and made his way through the sea of cowboys to the bar.

More people were arriving, and the bar was filling up fast. The dance floor was packed with line dancers, and a few couples were dancing the two-step counterclockwise around the perimeter. Everyone seemed to be having a good time, and he relaxed enough to grin.

Set in the middle of an upper level overlooking the dance floor was the solid wood bar. Seating rimmed the outer edges of the dance floor against the walls. The place had the country bar essentials including an electronic bull that was currently throwing a rider through the air and onto the well-padded floor within a ring.

He spied the team as he neared the bar and was headed in their direction when he felt something brush against his thigh. He spun around, but no one paid him any attention, so he carried on until it happened again. However, he'd been waiting for it this time and managed to grab hold, but what he got wasn't what he expected. He had a fist full of fur and released it immediately.

When he looked down, he saw Molly, Jeff's lab, standing beside him. "Hey, girl. Sorry about that."

Her long tail began to wag as she passed him and continued up to the bar. He watched in amazement as she jumped up on her hind legs and rested her front paws against the bar top and barked once in the area where the servers picked up their drinks.

Clay, the owner, leaned over and held out a five-pack of canned beer attached by plastic rings. Molly closed her jaws around the empty sixth beer ring, and once she had a hold of it, she lowered down to the floor and walked over to Jeff, who was still in the booth. People had gotten out of her way as she passed by. Clearly not the first time she performed that trick.

Now that was cool.

Fletch couldn't help but smile wide. Marshall wasn't so bad a place to settle. People seemed nice enough. No one had been outright homophobic when they saw Brick and Roman holding hands, and Tuck and Andy were a couple who'd lived in the area for some time. Of course, some stared, but he had yet to see overt anger or disgust.

Fletch wasn't naïve. He knew many people had learned to keep their faces schooled to neutral, and he expected someone would show their stripes.

Spence motioned to him as he got closer and pointed at something behind the bar. He turned to check out what his teammate was pointing at and ended up locking eyes with the man he'd been avoiding, working behind the bar with Clay. He was wearing a dark green button-down shirt, which showcased his broad chest. His snug black jeans were highlighted by a large, rectangular silver belt buckle that shined when the overhead lights hit it. This was the first time Fletch had seen the sheriff out of uniform and he had to pick his jaw off the floor.

The handsome man had locked on to him.

Shit. He should've taken up Jeff's offer to sit with them. Now, Marie's smug expression made sense. Fletch should have known he'd never be able to avoid the sheriff.

Chapter Five

Elias knew the moment Fletch saw him. It wasn't hard to read his expressions. Desire filled his eyes, but it was quickly replaced by frustration. He'd caused that, and he was damn well going to fix it. No more of this hot/cold bullshit.

He made his way over to Fletch at the same time he reached his friends at the end of the other side of the bar. "Hey, Fletch." Elias had to shout over the noise. "I'm happy to see you made it out."

"Couldn't miss Marie's party," Fletch replied, and Elias could feel himself getting lost in those hazel eyes. "Looks like a great turnout."

"Yeah, a lot of folks are here to celebrate Marie, along with the normal weekend crowd. What can I get you?"

"Bud."

"Bottle or tap?"

"Bottle."

"You got it," Elias said before taking a few steps back and pulling a Bud out of one of the coolers underneath the bar top. He opened it and handed it over. "First one's on me."

Fletch's eyes widened, and he said, "Thanks. How did you end up working the bar?"

"Clay's other bartender's having car trouble, so I stepped in until he manages to get here." It'd been the right thing to do, but it forced Elias to push back his plans a bit. After tonight, he intended to leave no doubt in Fletch's mind about his intentions.

A few people called out for drinks on the other side of the bar. "I'll be back soon."

***

"Did the sheriff buy me a drink?" Fletch asked, looking down at his beer.

"He did," Roman said. "When are you going to stop calling him 'the sheriff' and use his name?"

"I don't know his name."

"Well, shit. You guys are dragging your asses big time. It's Elias. And I have no idea why you're confused about him. The guy's sending signals as bright as neon signs."

"I'm not sure what's going on," Fletch said. "Maybe he's drunk?"

"He's drinking a bottle of water," Spence pointed out.

"The sheriff didn't buy us a drink," Shaw noted. "Where's my free beer?"

"You're not Fletcher," Brick said. "It looks like your sheriff isn't holding back anymore."

"That could change. It has before." Fletch wasn't falling for this again.

"Brother, is there no winning with you?" Roman asked. "Before you were upset the guy didn't invite you to go with him. Now, you're unsure because he's showing you he's interested."

"Never said I liked you, Mr. CEO." Fletch and Roman had a rough start considering the guy's father was the sleaze who went after Brick's property. However, it soon became obvious Roman wasn't like his father.

Roman laughed. "Yeah, you did. On my birthday."

"I take it back," Fletch grumbled.

"Too bad, I already know the truth." Roman smiled wide, and Brick pulled him closer. They were the perfect couple: love, respect, and loyalty. "Now, back to the subject at hand. Elias is into you. All that's left is figuring out what you're going to do about it."

What *was* he going to do about it? He took a long pull on his beer and gave a mental shrug. How about nothing? He was in the mood to see what Elias's next move was.

"Since I'm not needed here, it's time to dance," Shaw announced as he stood.

"You know how to line dance?" Roman asked.

"I'll figure it out," Shaw said with his usual confidence.

"They're going to eat you up and spit you out. I'd better go with you and give you a quick lesson," Roman told him. "I've been line dancing and two-stepping since I could walk."

"It can't be that hard," Shaw protested as he eyed the dance floor.

"Okay," Roman said as he stood as well. "Show me whatcha got."

"I will." Shaw raised his jaw and walking away with Roman following behind.

"I gotta see this." Brick downed the rest of his beer and headed off in the same direction, leaving Fletch and Spence at the bar.

"Let's watch Shaw make a fool of himself. Again," Fletch said before taking a pull of his beer.

A phone rang, and Spence dug into his pocket. He looked at the screen and said, "I'd better take this outside where it's quieter."

Fletch finished his beer and turned his attention to Elias, who was serving drinks and talking to people on the other side of the bar. People liked him and gravitated to him. To be expected with his friendly vibe, good looks, and open personality.

Fletch preferred not to speak overly much and took time to warm up to people. They were opposites, and he wondered if Elias was the yang to his yin.

"Is this seat taken?" A man with piercing blue eyes wearing a black Stetson asked from Fletch's left side.

"No."

"Thanks," he said and tipped his hat to him as he sat. "Good turnout for Marie."

"Yeah," Fletch replied. There were a ton of gifts stacked up on Marie's table.

"My name's Bryan Murray," he said while holding out his hand. "I own a ranch just outside town limits."

Fletch shook his hand and introduced himself. "Fletcher."

"Nice to meet you, and thanks for the seat. I didn't think I'd find one at the bar."

Fletch glanced over at the new arrival and noticed the black cane at his side. "No one offered you their seat. That's bullshit." People suck.

"Thanks for being offended on my behalf, but it's okay. I don't need to be treated differently," Bryan said with a kind smile. "Owning a ranch is tough, and sometimes the cattle play dirty."

"Is that how you were injured?" Fletch asked.

"What can I get you, Bryan?" Elias asked as he came to a stop on the other side of the bar.

"Hey, Sheriff. I'll have a Corona and a Bud for my new friend, Fletcher," Bryan replied.

Bryan seemed cool, so Fletch nodded at Elias. "Thanks."

Elias bent down then put their beers on the bar. "Here you go, guys," he said. "You driving tonight, Fletch?"

Fletch looked up into Elias's dark brown eyes and for a moment his world shifted. A lot of emotion was swimming in there. If he wasn't mistaken, Elias looked a little pissed off.

"I drove the team in, so yeah."

"I don't mind driving them home if he has too many," Bryan offered, and the muscle in Elias's jaw began to jump. His chest expanded and he looked...bigger. Taller.

"That's mighty nice of you, but I'll be the one taking him home." Though he sounded cool, there was a definite edge to his tone.

How did this turn into a pissing match? "Neither of you need to worry about how I'm getting home. This is my last beer. I'll be drinking water after that."

There, problem solved. Elias narrowed his eyes, shook his head, and went back to serving other customers.

Bryan raised his hands like he was surrendering. "Sorry, man. Didn't know you and Elias have a thing. I don't poach."

"Poach? We're not dating." *Wait a minute. Bryan's interested?*

Bryan looked across the bar to where Elias was standing, then back to Fletch. "Are you sure about that? 'Cause Elias's making his claim loud and clear."

Fletch shrugged. He wasn't going to get into it with Bryan. None of anyone's business, and Fletch wasn't sure there was anything to talk about.

"I'd still like to be friends. There's a small but strong LGBTQ community here in Marshall, and we're always happy to gain new folks."

"Good to know." And surprising. Not the type of area he would've pegged to have a gay community.

"I heard you and your team are all former Navy SEALs. Thank you for your service."

Fletch nodded. He never knew what to say when someone thanked him for doing his job. "You were about to tell me how you injured your leg."

"Rodeo." Bryan laughed. "The bull won."

"Bull riding? And I thought I was an adrenaline junkie. You couldn't pay me enough to hop onto the back of a two-ton bull."

"My mom figured all my good sense got knocked out of me after a particularly nasty run. I still have no idea how I held on for eight seconds." Bryan grinned and Fletch knew at that moment they'd be good friends.

"Is the prize money worth it?" he asked.

"For professionals, it can make them millions. But I'm no professional. Whatever prize money I make from local rodeos goes back into the ranch."

"Cool. You raise cattle?"

"Yep. Two hundred and twelve head. Texas Longhorns. Got about five hundred acres."

"Holy shit, that's a lot of horns." Those suckers were huge.

Bryan laughed. "Yep, it is. But we're nowhere near the biggest in the state. Far from it."

"For real. How big are their horns?" Fletch had only seen them in pictures.

"They can grow to over eighty to one hundred inches tip to tip for a male."

"For a male?"

"Yep. The cows have horns as well, but not as long as the bulls. They start growing them at three weeks."

"What starts growing at three weeks?" Shaw asked as he rejoined them at the bar.

"Longhorn cattle's horns," Fletch provided. "Bryan, this is one of my teammates, Shaw."

"Nice to meet you, Shaw," Bryan said as he held out his hand.

Shaw took hold immediately. "Same. Wanna dance?"

Leave it to Shaw to fly in and immediately hit on the man. Sometimes Fletch wished he had the same ballsy attitude.

"Sorry. Gonna take a rain check," Bryan said as he lifted his cane. "Got a couple more months' worth of healing to do first."

Shaw's demeanor didn't change. He grabbed an empty bar stool and plunked it down beside Bryan. "Tell me more about Longhorn cattle, cowboy. Would you like a beer?"

"Hey," Fletch grumbled. Shaw always took over every conversation. "Weren't you supposed to be dancing up a storm?"

"Do you want the sheriff to shoot him?" Shaw asked Fletch while gesturing down to the end of the bar.

Sure enough, Elias stood there with his arms crossed over his chest, watching the three of them like he had a right to be pissed off. For some reason, Fletch jumped completely out of character and mouthed, "Screw you."

Elias's right eyebrow shot up so fast Fletch wondered if he'd imagined it. Elias's eyes darkened, and he strode over until he stood directly in front of Fletch. "You have something to say?"

He shouldn't care, and he wasn't the type of person to jump first and ask questions later. He liked preparation and measured action. It'd saved his life more times than he could count. But Elias was on Fletch's last nerve, and he'd be damned if he'd back down.

"Yeah. I said, 'screw you,' and I mean it," Fletch growled low in his throat. "I'm tired of whatever game you're playing. If you aren't interested, back off."

"I never said I wasn't interested," Elias shot back.

"Really? Is it a covert mission, and I'm on a need-to-know basis?"

Elias was standing right in front of him and said, "Not anymore." He reached over the bar, wrapped his large hands around the back of Fletch's neck, and pulled him forward before taking his lips in a punishing kiss.

Fletch wanted to say he fought it, but since it was exactly what he'd wanted, he sucked Elias's tongue into his mouth and went all in. In this moment, he didn't give a fuck he was in a packed bar. He moaned into Elias's mouth, loving the feel of his soft lips pressed against his as their tongues explored deeper, and he got lost in the sensations running through his body.

Until he heard someone cough to his left before saying, "Fuckin' fags."

He and Elias pulled apart to confront the asshole. But it appeared he didn't have to. Shaw and Bryan were standing, and Brick,

Roman, and Spence were headed their way. The fishing crew was closing in fast.

Before a fist could be thrown, Clay yelled, "You can leave now, Frank Edwards, or I can have someone assist you in finding the door. I don't tolerate any of that bullshit in my bar. Don't bother coming back. That goes for anybody who has a problem. Leave now, or I'm sure a few of our country's finest can show you the way."

Edwards was speechless as he looked around for backup that wasn't coming. Fletch was shocked as well. He was positive others in the crowd felt the same way as Edwards, but they didn't want to risk being kicked out of the local watering hole.

"God made man and woman," Edwards yelled. "Not this abomination. It'll spread throughout the county if we don't stop them."

"Time for you to go," Jeff said as he came up behind the man.

Edwards jumped and spun around. "Don't come up behind me. I don't want you anywhere near my ass."

"Trust me. No one wants anything to do with your ass." Jeff stayed cool as the crowd laughed.

Edwards cocked his arm back, but a hand reached out and stopped him before he could throw the punch. It was hard to see who it'd been, but he was headed to the front door with a little help from the other townsfolk.

"I'd better go and make sure he leaves peacefully," Elias said as he released Fletch's hand. "I'm sorry I did that."

Before Fletch could ask what he meant, Elias was gone. What the fuck? What exactly was he sorry about? For making a scene or kissing him in the first place? Hell, he'd had enough of this second-guessing bullshit. Give him an in-country rescue deep in a South American jungle any day over this shit.

"I'm going out back to get some fresh air," he said to no one in particular. Since the action was located out front, he figured the back patio was a better option for getting a little space.

He walked across the now empty dance floor, out the back screen door, and onto the empty patio full of picnic tables. He'd have a few minutes of peace before the people returned to their seats. He heard a truck's tires squealing out of the parking lot and figured Edwards was gone.

In many ways, life had been easier as a member of a SEAL team. He knew the enemy, and his brothers had his back. Now, out among civilians, he felt like a duck out of water. He should've never left the Navy. Hell, he should re-up and get back to a world that made sense.

But… He couldn't go back without his team. Even if he felt left out in the open most of the time. He'd have to find cover and keep his head down. So much for fitting in. The first public event in their new community was a bust, and he'd been front and center of the action.

"Damn," he growled as he kicked a stone across the deck. "Everything's fucked up."

"I'd say that's about right, fag," an angry voice said from behind him.

Fletch spun around, pissed he hadn't heard Edwards coming. "Whatcha do? Park your truck and double back on foot?"

"Congratulations," Edwards said as he lifted a gun he'd had hidden behind his back. "You win the prize, freak."

Fletch looked at the Smith and Wesson revolver. A big, silver bastard with its shiny cylinder and barrel. The hammer was pulled back, and it had what looked like a mother-of-pearl grip. Had it ever been fired?

"Now you want to shoot me?" Fuck, his night was going from bad to insane.

"Hell yeah, before people like you have a chance to infest this fine upstanding community," Edwards said like he was the spokesperson for all of Marshall. "You couldn't keep it behind closed doors."

Fletch noticed the slight shake of the man's hand. "Have you ever killed a man, Edwards? Looked him in the eye as the life drains out of his body? Watched him gasp for his last breath while his lungs filled with blood?"

"Shut up," Edwards growled.

"Pointing a gun at a man isn't the same as a coyote." With every word, he slowly inched closer to the gun. Every move choreographed and unthreatening. "Can you feel the adrenaline running through your body at the power you hold? The life of a real person in your hands."

"I said shut up," Edwards yelled, punctuating every word with a shake of the gun.

"I've felt what you feel in this moment before pulling the trigger. Anger, the need to do what you believe is right. But is it right when your prize will be seeing my lifeless eyes in your nightmares? Every time you sit down and close your eyes, I'll be there. Taking a life will change you, and you can never go back to the way things were. There'll be no safe harbor for you. No returning home to your family. No more Sunday dinners or friends."

Fletch was only a couple of feet away, and Edwards was lowering his weapon. It was working. Talking Edwards down from his rage might get him out of there without injury. At least until a bloodcurdling scream from behind them caused them both to jump. When Edwards's hand flinched, his finger was still on the trigger and the gun went off.

Fletch felt the familiar searing pain when the bullet ripped through his left arm. The impact from the hand cannon threw Fletch off balance, sending him backward, and his head clipped a picnic table on his way down.

The last thing he remembered was staring up at the stars thinking he should've never left the Navy.

Chapter Six

Elias paced the waiting room at Marshall Medical Center, waiting for word about Fletch's condition. The rest of his team was there, filling the small area fast. Marshall didn't have a real hospital, but their medical center could handle most injuries. Full-blown traumas required a medevac, and the patients were transferred to a major hospital.

The clock on the wall read 2:54 am, and Elias's head had been pounding for hours. Seeing Fletch laid out on the ground bleeding from a bullet wound had shaken him to his core. Edwards had better hope someone else found him first.

"What's the deal, Sheriff?" Shaw asked breaking the silence.

"Deal?" He was waiting here with the rest of them.

"One minute you're all hot and heavy, eye-fucking Fletch, and then you're cold as ice."

"Eye-fucking? Shaw, that's a visual I could've done without," Roman huffed. "But it's a legitimate question. What's with the games?"

Elias knew Fletch's friends and team were looking out for him, but it grated on his nerves to be called out. Although, admittedly, he'd been behaving like a confused teenager with his first crush.

"That's between me and Fletch."

"Not anymore," Brick stated. "Your actions had consequences." His gaze darted to the swinging double doors down the hall.

"I know tonight's on me." Elias held himself personally responsible for Fletch getting hurt. He should've ensured Edwards didn't double back. He should've taken Fletch outside before making out like they were in high school.

"We're not saying you're responsible for what Edwards did," Shaw told him. "That's on him. What we're saying is telling Fletch it was a mistake kissing him before taking off fucked with his head."

"Mistake? I never said kissing him was a mistake." He'd never say that. Elias had loved every second and wanted more.

"Dude, I was standing right there when you said, and I quote. 'I'm sorry I did that,'" Shaw said. "Brutal shit."

Elias wracked his brain, and it came to him. "Okay, yeah. But I meant embarrassing him in front of everyone at the bar. If I'd controlled myself, none of this would've happened. I know I fucked up."

"Man, you've got to get better at this communication thing," Spence said. "You suck at it."

"I'll take that under advisement." When he saw Fletch, there'd be no more misunderstandings.

The double doors opened and Dr. Barbara Wright walked into the waiting area. Elias asked, "How is he?"

"Mr. Daniels will be fine, but we're going to keep him overnight for observation. He has a concussion. The bullet went into his left bicep muscle, and we removed it and set it aside for you, Sheriff, along with a report of his injuries. The bone was unaffected. We expect the muscle that sustained damage will heal without causing any impairment."

"Can we see him?" Brick asked while pulling Roman closer.

"Yes. He's in room three on the right. But don't stay too long. He needs to rest and recover," she advised. "If the next twelve hours goes well, we'll be able to release him by this afternoon."

"Understood." Brick led the team through the double doors and Elias hung back. He had more questions for the doctor.

"Are you sure there won't be any loss of motion to his arm?"

"I'm sure this man had been trained to within an inch of his life. He'll get back his full range of motion because he won't accept any other result."

"How long do you think it'll take him to heal?"

"Considering he's asking when he can leave, I'd say our biggest concern might be slowing him down enough to give his body time to heal."

"I'll make sure he does."

***

Fletch wanted out of this fuckin' white antiseptic room. He didn't need the movie reel of his last hospital stay on replay. The last place any servicemember wanted to be was in the med tent or hospital.

His arm was throbbing in its sling, which was his fault for refusing the pain meds. They always knocked him out, which was a no-go. His head pounded at a completely different pace, leaving him without a moment's peace.

He looked around and noticed he was alone. Never one to waste an opportunity, he slid his legs over the side of the bed. His clothing sat in a bag on a chair close to him. He could get out of this hospital gown and—

"Get your ass back in that bed." Brick's voice broke the silence and had Fletch backtracking. "Where'd you think you were going?"

"Away from here," Fletch said, even though he was getting back into the bed.

The team filed in behind Brick, and it didn't take long before his room was full and his chance for escape was lost.

"The doctor said you have to stay for observation. Suck it up, buttercup." Spence glanced at his cellphone screen. He'd been preoccupied all night with his phone.

"What's so damn important you've had your phone stuck to your hand all night."

His friend quickly pocketed his phone. "Sorry. Doing a bit of research."

"How are you feeling?" Roman asked as he rearranged the covers that'd gotten messed up on Fletch's failed bid at freedom.

"I'm fine. I can go home," he stated.

"Not going to happen," Roman told him as he tucked Fletch back in. "Now relax and get better."

"C'mon. I've already had the shittiest night possible. I'll never be able to sleep here."

"You're staying put until Dr. Wright releases you," a deep, familiar voice growled from the doorway.

What was Elias doing here? As he looked around at his friends for an answer, no one said a word, and Elias worked his way to the side of his gurney.

"It's time for me to go," Shaw said. "I'll give you a call tomorrow."

"Say hello to Bryan for me," Fletch jabbed, knowing full well those two had hit it off.

Then Shaw did the exact opposite of what Fletch expected. Instead of boasting about his latest conquest, he rubbed the back of his neck and said, "I don't know when I'll see him again."

Before Fletch could respond, a nurse came in and told everyone, "It's time to go. You can come back tomorrow."

"Okay, man," Brick said. "We'll be back to pick you up tomorrow."

"Try to get some rest," Roman followed.

"Don't worry about Edwards getting a second chance. I'm going to hang around outside the medical center in case he gets any more stupid ideas."

"Thanks, Spence." Fletch's gaze slid to Elias. "He got away?"

"Yeah."

Fletch nodded and watched as the team left his room. The moment Spence reached the door, he pulled out his phone again, but this time he showed Brick what was on his screen before they were both out of sight.

Elias was the only visitor left in the room. "Aren't you leaving?"

"No."

"Sheriff, this is for you." The nurse came back in and handed him a small plastic bottle like the ones pharmacists used for prescriptions. It had a bullet rolling around inside it.

Then it hit him. Of course Elias was here. He's the damn sheriff. This visit wasn't personal. This was him working on the case against Edwards.

"Thank you," Elias said before shoving it into his jacket pocket. "I'll take it in."

Fletch asked, "Do you need to take my statement or something?"

"It can wait."

"Then why are you here?"

"I'm here to clear up a few things, so you never have to ask that question again." Elias grabbed a chair and set it beside Fletch's bed then sat. "First, there's this," he said while taking hold of Fletch's hand. The contrast between his pale freckled skin and Cooper's beautiful ebony skin was outstanding. However, inside they were the same. Two gay men trying to find their way. "We have a lot to talk about, but in your condition you need your rest, so I'm only going to hit the high points."

"The high points?" Okay, Fletch had to admit his brain stuttered for a moment when Elias took hold of his hand. "And they are?"

"Okay. Yeah. I've been behaving erratically. But I want you to know without any doubt I'm interested in you. I want to go out on a date with you. A normal one that involves dinner and leads to a second date."

"Then why the hot and cold routine?"

"Beats the shit out of me." Elias buried his face into their joined hands. His skin was soft and warm, and Fletch couldn't help but run his finger along the handsome man's jaw, reveling in the feeling of his stubble. "I didn't want to come on too strong. You had only moved here a few months ago. Short time to have the sheriff lusting after you."

"You lust after me?"

Elias lifted his head and held his gaze. "Ah, yeah."

"When you told me about Marie's party, why didn't you ask me then?"

"I tried, and then I overthought it and didn't want you to feel like the team couldn't come. It all got mixed up."

Fletch couldn't help his angry tone when he asked, "Why did you tell me you shouldn't've kissed me?"

Elias reached up and cupped the side of Fletch's face. "I said I shouldn't have done that. I meant embarrassing you in front of the bar, which encouraged Edwards to start with his bullshit. I should've been able to control myself. But around you, everything gets twisted."

"You mean you liked kissing me?" Let's get that one thing straight.

"Hell yeah. I'd do it again if I didn't think you'd break my jaw."

"Try your luck." Fletch raised his eyebrow, daring Elias to follow through.

His eyes flew open, and he didn't waste a moment before he was leaning over Fletch and ran his calloused hand over the side of Fletch's face, causing goosebumps to rise across his arms. "You sure about this? 'Cause when I start, I don't intend to stop until I make you mine."

"Positive." Now that they were on the same page, Fletch was all in.

Fletch's head sunk into the pillow as Elias's lips covered his. This time Elias wasn't as forceful as he'd been during their first kiss, but Fletch was soon lost in the feel of Elias's lips, the glide of his tongue, and the taste of mint and coffee. Elias's big hands roamed over his chest, leaving a trail of fire everywhere he touched.

Too soon, the kiss slowed, and when he opened his eyes, his vision was filled with Elias's handsome face. His chocolate brown eyes shone with desire.

Now, this was what he was talking about.

And it only took him getting shot to figure it out.

Chapter Seven

Fletch stretched out on the lounger, took a pull off his beer, and watched the small waves breaking against the shore. He'd been home for one day and he was already in hiding from the well-wishers, helpers, and pseudo-doctors living with him in the lake house. They meant well, but they were driving him nuts.

He knew he was a horrible patient, and sure, his arm hurt. But it wasn't hanging off his body or gushing blood, which was the way everyone was acting. Elias had already stopped in twice and called once. Talk about what a difference a day makes: When the man was all in, he was all in.

"You sure you should be drinking beer?" Shaw asked as he came around the corner.

"I'm not on painkillers, so it's fine." Fletched moved his beer onto the other side of his chair in case Shaw got any crazy ideas.

"They didn't give you any at the hospital?" Shaw looked incredulous while tying his shoulder-length blond hair into a ponytail. "That's not right. You were shot."

"I didn't accept them," Fletch snapped. "I'm fine." He moved his beer a little farther away.

"Easy, man. I wasn't going to take it from you." Shaw sat in a nearby chair. "But I think I'll join you for a bit. It's sunny and quiet here."

"Rick being here have anything to do with that?" Fletch asked with a grin. Rick was Roman's assistant and best friend who was visiting from Dallas. He stayed with them every other week when Roman was at the lake house for more than five days. He and Shaw had a special kind of relationship: they drove each other nuts.

"The guy never lets up," Shaw huffed. "It's like he enjoys torturing me."

"He probably does." Fletch laughed.

Rick was a good guy and was cool with the rest of the team, but he and Shaw were like oil and water. Astonishing, considering they were so much alike personality wise, but not in stature. Shaw was over six feet and Rick barely broke five foot two inches. They both had an abundance of confidence, a razor-sharp wit, and quick mind, as well as an ego to match. Maybe they were more like repelling magnets than oil and water. Made of the same stuff, they couldn't coexist in the same space.

"Okay, okay," Fletch said at Shaw's exasperated look. "Let's talk about someone who makes you happier. Bryan. You guys seemed to hit it off the other night."

"Yeah, he seems like a decent guy."

Fletch waited for more, but Shaw stayed silent, not at all like his usual self. Something was up.

"And...?"

"Nothing." Shaw didn't look at him when he answered.

"Okay, what gives?" Fletch asked. "You're typically full of information about your latest conquest."

"He's not a conquest," Shaw clarified.

Fletch sat up higher in his chair. "Says the man who once told me that there was no man who could resist your charms once you set your mind on having them."

Before Shaw could answer, Fletch's phone rang. He looked at the screen, hoping it was Kyle, only to find Brick's name.

"Hey, boss, whatcha need?"

"Could you and Shaw come inside for a moment? We have some news." Brick's voice sounded not quite right, making alarm bells sound in Fletch's head.

"We're on our way." He knew better than to ask Brick for more information. If he said to come inside, that was where he'd tell them.

Fletch looked over at Shaw. "Brick needs us in the house. He has news."

"News about what? A new case?"

"Could be." Fletch stood and accidentally knocked over his beer. "Damn it."

"The fates are conspiring against you, my friend." Shaw laughed as Fletch retrieved the now empty bottle.

"Aren't they always." Sometimes it felt that way.

They made their way around the side of the house and Fletch noticed Elias's cruiser was back in the laneway.

"Looks like your man can't stay away," Shaw jabbed, causing Fletch to clamp his jaw tight. This attention was wonderful, but even he had his limits.

They climbed the porch stairs and walked into the living room through the garden doors. The entire team was waiting for them, along with Elias, Roman, Rick, and Julia. Yeah, they were about to hear something bad.

"What's wrong?" Fletch asked as they neared the waiting group. "Is it a new case?"

"You could say that," Brick stated, and those warning bells were growing louder by the moment. "We have news about Kyle."

"My brother?" Fletch asked. "What kind of news?" He noticed Elias moving closer until he was by Fletch's side, and he laid his hand on Fletch's shoulder. "What's happened?"

"When you told me it'd been days, and he hadn't called you back," Spence moved a little closer, "I decided to look into it because your brother always calls you back within forty-eight hours."

Fletch's mouth was so dry he could barely speak. "Is he dead?"

"No. Not from what I've been able to find. But he's missing and has been for over two weeks."

"Weeks? Why hasn't someone called me?" The moment the question was out of his mouth, he knew the answer. "My fucking family."

Elias squeezed his shoulder. "We'll find him." Fletch kept his eyes straight and his breathing regulated.

"Is there an active investigation going on in Seattle?" There had to be. He'd be on the first flight back, even though he hated going there.

"Yeah, but they don't have much to go on. Kyle was last seen on the twenty-first of last month by his assistant, and we haven't been able to reach him."

"Is that why you had your phone glued to your hand over the past couple of days?"

"Yeah. We got confirmation a few minutes ago. I didn't want to say anything without facts."

"We can be in Seattle by late this evening," Brick stated. "We're ready to go."

Fletch looked at his friends. Each ready to drop everything to help him find his brother. "Thanks, man."

***

Elias had packed before coming out to the lake house. Brick had given him the heads-up about heading to Seattle to find Fletch's brother, and there was no way he'd sit by while they searched. His officers could hold down the fort for a few days while he helped Fletch and his team.

Brick had told him that there was no love lost between Fletch and his family, but Kyle was different. That was all he knew. If his man needed him, he'd be there.

"Thanks for coming. You didn't have to," Fletch said as he zipped up his duffle bag. "I know we're new."

"A couple of days, a couple weeks or months, makes no difference." Elias walked over and took Fletch into his arms. "What matters is how we feel about our relationship. I'm all in, and that's all I need to know."

Elias enjoyed holding Fletch. It wasn't often he found someone as big as he was who'd allow being held. It always turned into a wrestling match for dominance. Not saying that Fletch wasn't dominant—Navy SEAL—but he allowed Elias to hold him in a way many men felt they were being subdued.

"My brother is the only one in my family who loves me even though I'm not a brainiac." Fletch shook his head as if to say, *It's no use even trying.*

"That's bullshit. You'd mentioned something about this when we talked during your run last week." There was no way in hell he'd allow Fletch to feel inferior. "You know, IQ scores don't make a man."

"Not according to most of them. I always had Kyle though." Fletch's voice turned rough with emotion. A brothers' bond was in jeopardy.

"We will find him. I swear it. We'll all move heaven and earth to see you two reunited," Elias promised. "I've made a few calls to old friends in Seattle. They'll help us to get where we need to be." Some of his old Marine buddies had settled there.

Fletch looked up to him and said, "Thanks, man. I appreciate it."

Elias gave him a gentle shake. "It's what I do when someone means something to me."

Fletch gave him a half-hearted smile. "You're being too good."

"Remember that when I inevitably piss you off."

Now he got a real smile. "Roger that."

Elias lowered his head to kiss Fletch when someone started banging on the bedroom door. "Saddle up. We're out of here in five," Spence yelled from the hallway.

"We'd better get going." Elias stepped back, but it seemed his man had other things in mind.

"Right. But first…" Fletch pulled him closer and dove in for a possessive kiss that promised so much more. Their bodies molded together as if they'd done this a thousand times. When they parted, both were gasping for air and sporting sizeable hard-ons.

Unfortunately, everything Elias wanted to do to and with Fletch would have to wait.

"Ready?" he asked.

"Yeah. Let's find my little brother."

Chapter Eight

Seattle was hot and sunny, a marked change from its normal rainy, gray bleariness. There was a heat wave working its way up the west coast into Canada. Instead of heading to the house they'd rented, they picked up the two SUVs at the car rental and went straight to the local police station where the missing person's report had been filed.

They'd talked to the desk sergeant, who contacted the chief, and then they were ushered into a small conference room to wait for Police Chief Roady to appear and give them a rundown on Fletch's brother's case. Since he was Kyle's brother the information flow was smooth, but brows were raised at the presence of his investigative team. Fletch didn't give a rat's ass what anyone thought. All he wanted was his brother back.

There was a knock on the door then a man walked in carrying a thin file. He wore a suit with his badge clipped to his belt, and his gun in its shoulder holster was visible under his jacket.

"Sorry to keep you waiting." He set the file down on the table in front of him. "I'm Police Chief Roady, and you're here about the Kyle Daniels case."

"Yes. Kyle is my brother," Fletch replied. "Do you have any leads?"

The chief opened the file and handed the information over. "We received a missing person's report from Mr. Daniels's assistant, a Mr. Franklin Davies."

He looked up from reading the file. "Not my family?" Fletch asked.

"No. When we contacted them, they stated they didn't know he was missing, especially since Kyle tended to take off now and then." Roady looked at his notes and nodded.

"Kyle doesn't take off." His family was way off base. They knew better and it pissed him off they told the cops what they had.

"Have there been any sightings?" Elias asked. "Have you had a chance to run his credit cards to check if he used them?"

"No sightings and his cards haven't been used. We searched his apartment. There were no signs of foul play. Everything was spotless, and his car was in his parking spot. We checked with the airlines, trains, and vehicle rentals around town and came up dry. It's as if he vanished."

"He's out there," Fletch said. "We need to find him. Someone or something is keeping him from contacting me."

There was another knock on the door and a large man with black hair walked in. The moment he and Elias saw each other, Elias stood. "Ray, good to see you, man."

"Hell, it's been years." Ray laughed and gave Elias a man-hug, then slapped him on the back a few times. Fletch kept his expression neutral, but inside he wasn't thrilled someone had their hands all over his man. Their relationship was new and he knew it was a knee-jerk reaction, but he didn't like the handsy shit. "Is this Fletcher?" Ray asked as they broke apart.

"Yeah. This is Fletch. My man," Elias said. And with that one phrase, Fletch felt himself relax. "Fletch, this is one of my old Marine buddies from way back in the day."

"Hey, man. Wish we were meeting under better circumstances," Ray said as he held out his hand.

"Good to meet you, Ray. Hopefully, we'll be able to find Kyle fast." Fletch wanted to make it clear that was the priority.

"We've assigned Detective Sommers to the case, and he will be your liaison with the police department going forward," Chief Roady announced. "He can take over from here. If you have any further questions Ray can't answer, please come to me."

Fletch had expected a little pushback from local LEOs, especially since the team came in together. But Roady and his crew treated them like colleagues. This must be what Elias meant when he said he'd be calling in a few friends.

Once Chief Roady left, Ray turned to Fletch and asked, "You haven't heard from your brother?"

"No. I've left several voice messages, but Kyle hasn't responded."

"And that's not like him?" Ray took out his notepad.

"No. It isn't. Kyle usually gets back to me within a couple of days."

"When was the last time you spoke to him?"

"About a month ago. Right after I decided to stay on at the lake house." Kyle had been happy Fletch had found a place to call home with his team.

"Did he seem odd, or agitated at all?"

"No. Kyle was celebrating the sale of his start-up. He'd worked hard to make that happen, and I was proud of him." Fletch remembered how excited Kyle had been and how plans were in the works for his next venture.

"Do you know of anybody who might target your brother?"

"Nobody that I can think of. I've been wracking my brain trying to think of anyone that might have a grudge against him, but he never complained of anyone. At least not to me."

"How about we pick this up at your parents' house in the morning. You can get more out of them than the officer did," Ray said.

"If we don't get the door slammed in our face, the best we can hope for is revulsion and derision. Don't be surprised if things spiral and full-on hate makes an appearance." Fletch ground his teeth.

"I'm takin' it you don't get along well with your parents," Ray said.

"We're estranged. I haven't spoken to my parents and my sisters in years. Kyle is different. He never cared about me not being like the others."

Ray blinked, tilted his head and asked, "Care to clarify that?"

"Black sheep. Not intelligent enough. Most likely to be blown up out in the field. You name it, and I've disappointed them."

"Gotcha. Well, that could work in our favor," Ray said with a gleam in his eyes. "I assume they don't know you're here looking into Kyle's disappearance."

"Right." Like he'd bother to call them.

"Good. Let's shake 'em up a bit. They're entirely too calm about your brother's disappearance, and it bothers me."

"You thinking they're involved somehow?" Brick asked, making Fletch's stomach flip.

"Possibly. I never rule anyone out without proof they weren't involved," Ray stated.

"We've tried to reach Kyle's assistant but haven't been able to track him down," Spence said.

"He hasn't come here since the day he made that report. We haven't needed to re-interview him." Ray looked down at the file.

"That's odd," Brick grumbled.

"You bet it is," Ray agreed. "I'll have a black-and-white swing by his apartment to check in on him."

"Thanks," Elias said.

"Let's get settled in at the house and try to get some sleep before we meet up with Fletch's family tomorrow," Brick said, but as always, it was a veiled order. "I have a feeling we'll need fresh eyes on this situation."

"Agreed," Ray said then looked to Fletch. "We'll meet up here before going on to your parents' house."

Fletch couldn't imagine how and why his parents would be involved in Kyle's disappearance. He was their golden boy. The young, rich entrepreneur who was the poster boy for all they believed their family represented. They'd have nothing to gain.

***

Less than an hour later, Fletch and Elias were lying in bed in the four-bedroom house they'd rented near the police station. He hadn't been in this city since college and never thought he'd be back.

"Try to get some rest, Fletch," Elias said while pulling him in closer. "You'll need your strength to deal with whatever happens tomorrow."

"I haven't seen them in over twenty-five years." He wondered what they'd look like, and if time had been kind to them. He was certain they'd be surprised at how he'd changed. All for the better. Even though he was battle hewn and unafraid, they wouldn't notice his confidence and how well he knew his abilities. His team knew, and they were the family he chose so they were the only ones who mattered.

Regardless of their reaction, he'd bulldoze through any hurdles they put in front of him to get his brother back. The odd thing was he wasn't as nervous about their reunion as he thought he'd be. He viewed them as a nuisance rather than all-powerful as he had when he was young.

"You're not alone," Elias assured. "The team and I will have your back."

"Thanks, but I don't think they'll make a scene with the detective there. They've always been overly concerned about their image within the affluent Denny-Blaine community." It wouldn't look good for two highly acclaimed professors to lose their shit in public.

Fletch stretched out his left leg and laid it over Elias's while his head rested on the big man's chest. They were both wearing their boxer briefs, and Elias filled his damn well, but this wasn't the time for further exploration.

"You said your parents found Kyle an acceptable member of the family because his IQ was high. Why aren't they more worried about his disappearance?"

"It would require them to show emotion, which is illogical to them." God, he sounded like he was talking about a sci-fi character, but the truth was the truth.

"WTF? Seriously, they're that messed up?"

Fletch nodded. "You'll see firsthand tomorrow."

He remembered when his mother was contacted regarding his grandmother's death. She went through the motions of being a loving daughter when they were at the funeral home, but she was on the phone with the estate lawyer the moment it was over.

"Charming. I can't wait," Elias groaned before turning off the bedside lamp. "Now, rest."

"Are you always this bossy?"

"Only when it comes to work, you, and your welfare."

"You know I'm a Navy SEAL, right?"

"I'm well aware you can take care of yourself, but it doesn't mean I can't care about you and do what I can to keep you safe."

Fletch thought he wasn't a lesser man by allowing it, and he'd do the same if the shoe was on the other foot.

"That role is interchangeable."

"Exactly. You get it," Elias said.

"If the roles were reversed, I'd be behaving like you are."

"It's not about who's more dominant. It's about what each of us needs at a specific moment," Elias explained.

Fletch angled his head up instead of pushing himself, but the request was the same. A kiss. Elias didn't hesitate before leaning down and kissing him long and slow.

When the kiss ended, he laid his head on Elias's chest and listened to his strong and steady heartbeat. He tracked the rhythm and it calmed him.

As his eyelids began closing he swore, *I'll find you, brother.*

Chapter Nine

Elias watched as they drove past mansion after mansion as Lake Washington glimmered in the distance. They'd left his tax bracket several neighborhoods back, but it didn't bother him. Status never did.

"Wow, nice neighborhood," Spence chuckled as they turned the corner. They were following Ray's car through the winding, tree-lined streets.

"Isn't this where Kurt Cobain used to live?" Shaw asked from the backseat.

"Yeah. He shot himself in the greenhouse behind his home," Fletch answered. "I was a teenager when it happened."

"Sad to believe you're at a point where you can't see your way out," Shaw muttered.

"I felt bad for his wife and daughter," Spence said. "It's always the ones left behind who pay the price."

Elias felt there was more behind Spence's comment, but now wasn't the time to figure him out. They were on a mission to find Kyle Daniels, and that would remain his focus until the job was done.

"We're close now," Fletch said with a distinct lack of emotion. The tension instantly ramped up a couple more notches inside the SUV.

Elias squeezed Fletch's knee, hoping to reassure him. This whole scenario had to be a nightmare for him coming back here after all these years to confront the people who'd turned their backs on him.

Their vehicle began to slow before turning into a long, paved lane leading to what looked like a large-scale Tudor-style house. The brick exterior had steeply pitched rooves, multiple front-facing gables decorated with half-timbers and stucco. Two large chimneys were as bookends on either side of the house, while the windows had diamond-shaped panes of glass.

The lawn was expertly manicured, not a blade of grass out of place. The trees were trimmed equally meticulously, and a patch of Douglas firs surrounded the property, giving the house privacy on three sides. It was so perfect it felt almost sterile.

"You used to live here, man?" Shaw asked in the same tone he used when discussing the late singer. Elias didn't miss his empathy.

"Yeah," Fletch huffed. "Home sweet home."

They parked their vehicles in front of the house, and everyone got out without saying a word, and quietly, they surrounded Fletcher.

Ray came over. "Ready to shake things up?"

"As I'm ever going to be," Fletch responded without emotion. He was shutting down. Throwing up walls to protect himself before seeing his parents.

"You're not alone," Elias whispered.

With a nod, the detective led them toward the front door. Elias noticed Shaw and Spence breaking off from their group, both rounding either side of the house. Their mission was to look for anything unusual. So far, their group was the only thing unusual in this neighborhood.

"Fletch, I'd like you to knock on the door. Is that okay?" Ray asked.

He nodded. Elias didn't like the entire situation, but they had to start somewhere to find Kyle, and shocking the shit out of his family might do it.

Ray stepped back with Brick and Roman while Elias followed Fletch up to the door. Without hesitation, he knocked on the polished wood and took a step back.

"Coming," a female voice yelled from inside the house.

Elias didn't miss the tremble working its way through Fletch's body. He would stay by his side throughout whatever horror lay on the other side of the door. If they thought they could pull the same bullshit on Fletch now, they had another thing coming.

***

Fletch dragged in a ragged breath and waited for the door to open. He never imagined himself in this situation since he'd had no intention of ever coming back here. His mind raced with outcomes, from having the door slammed in his face to his father going to get his gun.

The clicks of the locks being unbolted set his nerves on edge, but he refused to give them the satisfaction of seeing anything but who he was. Strong, and he had his chosen family with him no matter what.

The brass doorknob turned, and the thick wooden door was slowly opened. An older woman with her gray hair pulled up into a severe bun looked at him with shrewd blue eyes. Fletch sensed the moment she recognized him.

"Hello, Mother." His words came out flat.

Without even saying a word, she reached for the edge of the door to slam it shut when Ray made his appearance.

"Hello, Mrs. Daniels," he said. "I hope this isn't a bad time. I'm Detective Sommers with the Seattle PD. I've been assigned Kyle's case."

She stopped at the sight of the detective. "Detective Sommers, what can we do to help?" Fletch almost laughed. She wanted to help like she wanted to chop off a limb.

"I have a few more questions regarding Kyle's disappearance, and I ran into your other son Fletcher here and the team he brought along to help find his brother. I'm sure you of all people would welcome the extra help." The detective kept his voice friendly and conversational.

Damn, Ray was smooth. If dear old mom shut the door now, it would look suspicious, and refusing to accept extra help would appear odd, and would bring a whole lot more attention to them from law enforcement's point of view.

"We've told you everything we know already, detective. We wouldn't want to waste any more of your time." She was trying to get out of this meeting.

Ray came to stand beside Fletch. "It's never a waste of time to find your son, ma'am. We wouldn't want to leave any stone unturned, right?" His voice had changed slightly, becoming sterner as he stared directly at her. "Your missing son has to be your number one concern at a time like this."

She consented and opened the door fully as Fletch's father walked into the foyer and stopped dead in his tracks.

"What's going on?" he demanded. "What are you doing here?" If looks could kill, Fletch would be writhing on the ground in pain while his life slipped away.

"Detective Sommers is here to ask more questions, and Fletcher has come to help find Kyle," she quickly stated. Her tone made it clear she didn't want dear old dad losing his cool in front of the law.

Fletch watched as emotions played across his father's face, and he did not disappoint. "Why would you think you could find Kyle, considering far more intelligent people have tried and no one else has succeeded? Don't embarrass yourself. You're not needed here."

Fletch felt the group vibe, and he had to hide his grin. They couldn't think there would be anything they could say or do that would intimidate him. He waited to feel all the things they'd worked so hard to make him feel right up 'til the day he left. But nope. Nothing. Everything was different now, and he wasn't all that surprised he didn't feel a thing. Anger and frustration that they seemed unconcerned about Kyle, sure. But that was it. And it was all they were going to get from him. They'd tried to take away everything a family was supposed to give a child, but Kyle rejected them when he stood by Fletcher. For that alone, Fletch would do anything to find his brother.

"Sorry, Chuck, but I'm not going anywhere," Fletch stated. "You have no idea who you're dealing with."

His father looked stunned for a moment but quickly recovered. "That's Charles to you."

Now that he had his attention, it was time to lay it on. "Sorry, Charlie, but we have questions. Let's get this over with quickly because I don't want to be here way more than you don't want me here. I find your behavior…distasteful."

Elizabeth, his mom, looked shocked and glanced past them toward the neighbors' house before waving to someone. "Charles, the Biedermans are out in their flower garden."

"Maybe I should go over and say hello," Fletch threatened. "It's been a lot of years since I last visited. Do you think they'll remember me? Maybe they know what's going on around here." The more he spoke, the stronger he felt.

His father looked like he'd bit into a lemon. "Fine, come in, but don't touch anything," he huffed before turning away and heading in the direction of the formal living room.

Detective Sommers smiled wide and led the group.

Elias looked at Fletch, who shrugged. "No big. This shit ends here." He could either rise above or let them take him down all over again. He'd fought hard to be the person he was, and there was no way he'd step back.

Elias's smile was wide and meant so much more to Fletch than anything in this house of horrors. Once he found his brother, he and Elias could start behaving like they had a normal relationship, if possible.

When they walked through the entrance, Fletch couldn't dismiss the feeling of being watched, and it wasn't coming from his parents' glares. He looked to Brick, and with a subtle nod, Brick confirmed he felt it as well. When they were out in the field, they'd learned to listen to those gut feelings. Frequently, your hind brain and your body set off an alarm saying, you can't see it but it's there. It had saved their lives more time than any of them could count.

As they walked through the first level, he noticed subtle changes in the house. The Ming Dynasty vase with its vivid blue dragon was no longer displayed under glass for all to see. Elizabeth's prized Carrack china was no longer in the antique Italian display cabinet.

Other things began catching his attention, like the lack of fresh flowers adorning every room of the house as his mother had arranged with the local florists. Also, a few key paintings were missing from the hallway walls and a large one over the fireplace. His father had harped at him every time they'd pass one, reminding him that it was worth more than he was.

"Won't you have a seat," Elizabeth said while distinctly ignoring Fletch as if he weren't even in the room. When he was younger, he preferred it that way because then they weren't focusing on him. But Fletch was a man who'd spent a large portion of his life protecting others, and he demanded his due.

"Thank you, Elizabeth," Fletch said as he sat on one of his father's favorites, a "King-something-or-other" chair. He went as far as wiggling his ass on the cushion as he sat. The detective wanted to shake things up, Fletch could do that without even breaking a sweat.

Charles looked like his eyes were going to explode out of his head. The last thing his father had ever expected was seeing Fletch again, let alone having him sitting in front of them. It was time to use that to his favor because the only thing that mattered was Kyle.

Elias sat in a chair beside him while Ray, Brick, and Roman sat on the couch against the far wall. Charles and Elizabeth sat on an opposing loveseat.

The moment he saw his father suck in a deep breath, Fletch cut him off before he could start with his shit. "Where's Kyle?" Fletch asked. "What did he do to piss you off so much that you don't even care, or is it that you know exactly where he is?"

His father's mouth dropped open. In the past, Fletch wouldn't dare to speak to them like this, but it no longer mattered what they wanted, expected, or liked.

"What is the meaning of this, Detective Sommers?" Elizabeth feigned outrage as she fluttered her hand over her chest.

"Only questions, I assure you. Now when was the last time you saw your son Kyle?" Ray carried on as if nothing were out of the ordinary.

"We told you, one week before he disappeared," Charles replied in a tone that dared them to find something wrong.

Challenge accepted. "Is that seven calendar days or five workdays?" Fletch wanted clarification.

When they didn't answer, Ray reiterated, "Five or seven?"

Elizabeth answered, "Five."

"Hmmm, well, that's a difference of two days. A lot can happen in forty-eight hours," Elias stated. "Did you specify that last time you were interviewed?"

"Who are you?" Charles demanded instead of answering.

"Oh, excuse me, I forgot to introduce everyone," Ray said. "That is a colleague of mine, Sheriff Cooper."

"Sheriff." Charles' voice was noticeably hostile.

"And the other two men are part of LH Investigations, Brick and his partner Roman," Ray continued.

"You hired an agency to find Kyle?" Charles gave him a withering look. "Couldn't do it on your own?"

"Why would I? They're my business partners, and the sheriff here is my man." He reached out and grasped Elias's knee. "My family is here to help and support me."

The look on his parents' faces was priceless. It was a cross between shock and horror. He would've paid good money to see them like this, their feathers all ruffled. Not a smug look to be found.

"Back to the question, did you specify five or seven days in the initial interview?" Ray asked.

"I don't remember," Elizabeth said as if the information wasn't important.

"Do you remember what you and Kyle talked about?" Ray continued.

"He was depressed he had nothing to look forward to after selling his company," Charles provided.

"Funny, I spoke with him a month ago, and he was excited to be starting a new venture," Fletch said. "So why are you lying?"

"You may think you knew your brother, but you didn't," Charles shot back. "He was fragile, and we're worried he may have done something to himself."

"Now you're saying he was suicidal," Brick asked while Roman took notes. "Did you tell the authorities about your fears?"

"What are you writing down?" Elizabeth asked Roman.

"The inconsistencies in your statements. Do carry on," Roman said nonchalantly, and Fletch wanted to laugh. He was a cool CEO, that's for sure.

"No, but we offered to get him help," she explained. "He refused."

"What kind of help?" Ray asked.

"A psychiatrist," Charles said.

"Why didn't you tell the initial interviewer about his mental state during the interview?" Ray asked, looking her straight in the eye. As if daring her to lie.

She broke eye contact first. "We didn't want to embarrass Kyle and ruin his reputation."

"The only reputations the two of you are worried about are your own," Fletch said. "Is there anything else you haven't told the police? A few of Kyle's friends stated he'd been spending time in South Park. What do you know about that?" It was in the file he'd read from interviewees.

She didn't answer.

Ray shook his head. "If you make me re-ask the question, you might not like the way I pose it."

"Fine. He liked to hang out at a bar in South Park," Elizabeth said while waving her hand in the air as if shooing a fly away. "Big deal."

"Do you know the name of the bar?" Fletch asked as calmly as he could. Why wouldn't they have told the investigators everything the first time around?

"It was some Mexican place, on Fourteenth Avenue South, but I don't know the name." *Of course, she didn't.* "He liked slumming."

"Is there anything else you might have missed, no matter how insignificant you think it might be?" Ray prodded as he continued to write in his notebook.

"No, that's it," Elizabeth answered.

"Now, I have to ask you to leave. Any further questions will be answered through our lawyer," Charles blustered and stood, doing his lord of the manor thing.

That wouldn't do.

"You don't mind if we have a look around first, do you?" Fletch asked as he stood towering over the man who'd often claim there'd been a mix-up in the hospital nursery.

"What? Why would you want to look around?" Charles snarled through clenched teeth.

"I'm curious to see what else is missing around here," Fletch said, and he watched as fear crossed Charles's face. "So far, I've cataloged several prized pieces and family heirlooms."

"Get out," Charles yelled as he advanced on Fletch. Job complete.

Before Elias could move, Fletch motioned him back. He'd deal with Charles Daniels himself. He pulled himself up to his full height and flexed his muscles.

His father pulled back his arm, and when Charles threw the punch, Fletch easily grabbed his wrist, spun him around, and jerked his arm up his back. Target subdued.

"I'm not that frightened boy anymore, Dad," he said before shoving his father away. "I know something is going on here, and I won't rest until I find out what that is."

Fletch turned his back on them, as they'd done to him in the past, and walked away. When he reached the front door, he yanked it open and walked out into the sunlight, instantly feeling a whole hell of a lot better the farther he got from the house. The team caught up with him as he reached the SUV where Shaw and Spence were waiting.

"How did that go?" Shaw asked while scanning their faces.

"Better than expected," Ray said from behind Fletch. "We received new information and almost gave the old guy a heart attack."

Elias wrapped his hand over Fletch's shoulder, and he couldn't help but sink into the care. Now that the confrontation was over, he felt exhausted and wanted to be far away from their house.

"Can we finish this up at the rental?" Elias asked. "The sooner we're away from here, the better." He seemed to know exactly what Fletch needed.

Everyone agreed, and they were back on the road in no time. The SUV was silent as Fletch decompressed, thankful his teammates understood and gave him the room he needed. He had to get things straight in his head.

He would find his brother and figure out what was going on behind the scenes of his parents' Tudor fortress.

Chapter Ten

Elias fixed himself and Fletch fresh coffees as the team pored over everything they'd seen and heard that morning. Ray and Roman were taking notes so that nothing was missed, and everyone agreed what the Danielses had said seemed off.

"I swear it was empty," Spence stated while holding up three fingers in the unmistakable boy scout salute.

"You were never a boy scout," Shaw pointed out.

"Both the pool and the garage?" Brick asked, looking as confused as Elias felt. In this extreme heat, a pool would be a dream.

"Yep. Looked like no water had been in that pool for a couple of years, and there were no other vehicles in the detached five-car garage. It was empty. The only vehicle on the property, other than ours, was the Bentley in the driveway," Spence said while he typed away on his laptop, searching for something.

"My father had an extensive car collection," Fletch said. "This doesn't make sense. There was a '48 Jaguar XK120, an '84 Ferrari Testarossa, a '66 Ford Mustang, and a '69 Dodge Charger."

"That's one hell of a memory for over twenty-five years ago," Ray stated with a healthy dose of skepticism.

"It happens when you're forced to wash and wax them, polish the chrome until it shined, and prepare them all for inspection every month. If there was one thing out of place, real or imagined, I'd have to redo them all."

"Got it," Ray said as he cringed.

Elias wanted to punch something. "You and your siblings?"

"Nope. Only me. Charles said it would prepare me for my future employment opportunities," Fletch said without emotion. Every time Elias thought he'd heard the worst of what these people had done, something even more disturbing came up.

"Maybe he decided on a new hobby," Shaw suggested, "and the pool is no longer a priority for them."

Elias noted Fletch's team worked well together because they looked at a question from all sides.

"True," Fletch agreed. "Anything is possible."

"Or they're broke," Elias suggested as he handed Fletch his coffee. "Other things were missing. They could be selling it off over time when needed to pay the bills."

"I'll have their financials by morning," Ray stated as he picked up his phone.

"No need, I have them right here," Spence said before turning his screen around for the others to see. "They're still both pulling in low six-figure salaries from the private university they teach at, but all their investments and savings accounts have been closed for over three years."

"How did you get that information?" Ray asked, looking more than a little shocked.

Spence pointed at himself and said, "Information specialist trained by the Navy SEALs. There isn't much I can't find or do."

Ray shook his head. "That's scary on so many levels."

"At least I'm one of the good guys," Spence said before mumbling under his breath. "Today."

"How can they not have money? They'd inherited over two and a half million dollars when my grandmother died. I was a senior in high school and remember the number because my parents shouted it out when they received a copy of the will. Soon after, I left for college and never came back."

"Assholes," Shaw grumbled, and Elias had to agree.

"Total assholes," he added.

"I'll see what I can dig up with our CIs. If it's anything newsworthy, they might have heard something," Ray said. "Drugs, gambling, and the rest doesn't stay secret for long when that amount of money is involved."

"What about the bar in South Park they said Kyle liked to frequent?" Roman asked. "Are we going to go there? Could they be lying?"

"You bet we are," Fletch said. "I'll follow every lead no matter how slim. Besides, it was only when my mother was confronted by Kyle's friends' statements that she even mentioned the area."

"How many Mexican bars and restaurants are on Fourteenth Avenue South anyway?" Shaw asked.

"More than a few," Ray answered. "It'll take a day or more to visit each of them."

"I'll organize a list, and we can get started first thing tomorrow," Spence said as his fingers flew across his keyboard. There was nothing he couldn't do.

"I'd like to go to my brother's apartment to have a look around," Fletch told the group. "Can we go there this afternoon?"

"Yeah. I'll arrange it with the building manager," Ray stated. "Maybe new eyes can pick out something that may have been missed or doesn't belong."

"We have a plan," Elias said. "It's a start."

"We'll find Kyle, man," Brick stated. "I swear it to you."

Fletch looked around the room at each person. His thanks was plain to see in his hazel eyes. After a few moments and with a decisive nod, he stood.

"Let's go get my brother."

***

Fletch stood frozen at the threshold of Kyle's apartment, shocked at what lay before him. The place had been ransacked. Nothing was untouched. Furniture was flipped over, and drawers had been emptied onto the floor. Even the light fixtures were removed, leaving only the bulbs.

"I thought you'd said his apartment was spotless," Elias stated from over his shoulder. "Am I right in saying the apartment didn't look like this the last time the police were here?"

"Yeah. What the hell is going on?" Ray snapped. "Everyone stay out in the hall. I'm calling it in." Ray got on the phone and ordered a forensics team to the apartment. When he stuffed his phone into his inside jacket pocket, he sighed loudly and said, "Where's that damn building manager?" Then he walked off and headed down the hallway.

Fletch leaned in. He knew better than to compromise a crime scene. And even though the team was trained in how to go through the apartment without disturbing anything, he didn't want any of them to somehow taint evidence. From the front door, they were able to make a few important observations.

"They were looking for something," Fletch said. "Let's hope they didn't find it." He leaned to the left as far as his body could go and saw every kitchen drawer and cupboard had been left hanging open with its contents scattered across the counters and floors.

"Sometime between the officers' initial visit after Kyle was reported missing and now," Brick said, "someone tossed this place thoroughly."

"The door was locked from the outside. There was no forced entry," Shaw said. "I'm guessing they had a key or picked the locks."

Fletch's brother lived in a modest two-bedroom apartment in an average neighborhood even though he was worth tens of millions of dollars. This didn't make sense, and nothing about what he knew about his parents' financial troubles, along with Kyle's businesses, made sense.

Wait, worth millions. "What if he was kidnapped for his money?"

Brick grunted. "It's a theory. We can't count out any possibility."

Fletch felt sick to his stomach. His younger brother could be out there fighting for his life. "He's never hurt anyone."

"Do you think whatever they were looking for is gone?" Roman asked.

"Well. Whoever this was trashed everything we can see, and I'm guessing that's true throughout the apartment. I'd like to think they would've stopped once they found what they wanted. But this," Brick said while he scanned the wreckage, "leads me to believe they didn't,"

Fletch stared at the living room. The couch cushions were cut open along with the chair, and the stuffing was torn out. Framed pictures lay smashed against the hardwood floor, and the wall unit was overturned, the flat-screen shattered. He spotted a picture of the two of them in San Diego from last year's visit.

The frame lay in pieces as shards of glass encircled their smiling faces. Kyle had spent a week with him, and they'd traveled up the coast to Monterey. That road trip was great, and knowing Kyle had framed the snap confirmed it'd been special for his brother too.

He loved Kyle and couldn't stop from getting choked up. Elias must've sensed him losing it and came beside him, squeezing his bicep. Fletch shook his head as he put his hand over Elias's. "Sorry, I need to get my shit together and stay strong for Kyle."

"Showing emotions isn't a weakness. It's the most natural thing to do when faced with a bad situation. You aren't like your parents. You're warm, caring, and loyal. Don't ever be sorry for feeling."

"What could he have gotten into? Who the hell would trash his place? Instead of getting answers, I'm only coming up with more questions."

"We'll get those answers for you," Elias promised. He smiled wide and he kissed Fletch lightly on the lips. A kiss filled with caring and support, exactly what Fletch needed. He looked back at the picture and noticed something odd.

"What's that?" He pointed to a tip of a piece of paper sticking out from behind the smashed picture.

Elias leaned forward and couldn't make out what it was. "Spence, do you have anything that extends with tweezers or something like them in your bag of tricks?"

The team turned to see Spence crouched in front of the duffle he'd slung over his shoulder when they'd gotten out of the SUVs. He dug around for a moment and took out a compact trash collection device. He flicked a latch below the handle, and the arm extended out about three feet. At the end of the arm was a large plastic pincher, which was controlled at the handle.

"That's not gonna reach," Shaw said.

"Fletch," Brick called, "put Spence on your back and lean in as far as you can. We'll anchor you, and Spence can get up on your shoulders and lean in with the arm."

Easy. They'd stood on each other's shoulders to look over rocks in hostile territory, or over trees in jungles. This wasn't a big deal.

Brick circled Fletch's waist, then he leaned all the way forward, Spence climbed on his back, and got his knees on Fletch's shoulders. Someone had to be anchoring Spence 'cause he leaned forward as far as he could go before he released the arm and flung it out. They were able to slide the small piece of paper, no more than an inch wide, out from underneath the picture. Then the pincher grabbed hold of it and Spence retracted the arm. With Brick still holding him, Fletch crouched and Spence slid down. When Fletch turned, Shaw was handing Spence tweezers, which he used to open the paper.

His heart was trying to beat its way out of his chest as he read what was written: "24-17-35."

"Looks like a combination," Fletch said.

"To what?" Shaw asked.

"That's the million-dollar question," Brick answered.

Footsteps were coming toward the apartment. Fletch quickly pulled out his phone and took a picture of the paper before Ray and the landlord returned. Who knew how long it would take to process the scene? At least with a picture of the numbers, they could carry on with their investigation.

Spence put the paper between the pinchers, dropped the arm to its full length, then flicked the paper into the living room. It landed not far from the photo and was obvious. The crime scene techs wouldn't miss it.

No sooner had Fletch thought of them, a forensics unit arrived and there was no reason for them to stand out in the hall waiting hours for the techs to process the scene. Fletch wanted to do something productive, so they parted ways with Ray, who had to stay at the scene, and returned to their rental. There was still a lot of work to do.

Spence was busy compiling a list of every restaurant and bar in South Park. Elias was busy checking in with Marie to make sure all was good back in Marshall. There was still no sign of Edwards since the night he shot Fletch. Brick and Roman left to pick up food, and Fletch and Shaw sat on the couch trying to figure out where the lock was for this number combination.

Fletch looked down at the phone screen. "24-17-35. Where have I seen this before?"

"You recognize those numbers?" Shaw asked.

"There's something familiar about them, but I can't put my finger on it." Fletch knew the sequence somehow. He'd seen it, but couldn't remember where.

"If they don't find a safe in his apartment or at his office," Shaw said, "maybe it's a safety deposit box or a locker somewhere."

"Have they found Kyle's assistant yet?" Fletch asked.

"Ray said Franklin wasn't at his apartment when they went over earlier, and by the looks of things, he hasn't been there in several days," Spence told them without taking his eyes off the computer screen. "Papers have been piling up."

"Why would he be missing too?" Shaw asked.

"Maybe he's involved in Kyle's disappearance," Spence answered. "Or he knows something, and it has him running scared."

"Then why would he report Kyle as missing?" Fletch asked. It didn't make sense to go to the cops if he was involved.

"Clearly things aren't adding up," Shaw said what Fletch was thinking.

His brain was pounding. He was concentrating so hard on his phone screen, staring at the numbers he knew had to be important. He was pissed he couldn't remember where he saw them. What was the significance of hiding the combination behind a picture of the two of them last year?

His brother's disappearance was beginning to have more twists and turns than a roller coaster. Fletch knew in his gut that all this had some connection to his parents, which disgusted him. Since Kyle was one of the golden children, what happened to erase his standing?

Tomorrow Fletch would hunt down answers in South Park. If anyone knew anything, Fletch would find it.

Chapter Eleven

They'd been to every single bar and restaurant on their half of the list, and they'd come up empty. They'd even canvassed people on the streets and in stores. Fletch, Cooper, and Shaw started at one end of Fourteenth Avenue South near the South Park Bridge, while Brick, Roman, and Spence took the other end starting at South Director Street. Ray was still busy investigating who broke into and trashed Kyle's apartment.

The area they were canvassing had a large Hispanic community, one of the largest in the city. It was a mix of industrial, commercial, and residential that ran along the polluted Duwamish River. Most residences were single-family, but generations lived in the small homes and the neighborhood was tight-knit. Word of their arrival had spread quickly.

Fletch leaned back against the side of the SUV to regroup before starting all over again because he wasn't leaving here without some answers. He'd forgone wearing his sling. It only got in the way, and he could handle the pain. He'd had worse. Much worse. They'd been combing through the neighborhood since early that morning, and now the sun sat low in the sky. They'd brought along several pictures and had shown everyone they came across, but they hadn't turned up anything.

Another day wasted, and he was no closer to finding his brother. Desperation was starting to seep in no matter how hard he tried to fight it. Kyle had been gone for weeks before Fletch knew he was missing. Time was of the essence in kidnappings, and they were running out of it, if it wasn't too late already.

Fletch shook his head, rejecting the thought as it entered his mind. Kyle was alive, and he would find him.

Elias stood in front of him, giving him some privacy from curious passersby. The man was remarkably intuitive. Whatever Fletch needed was handled without him ever asking. It was like the handsome sheriff had a direct line to Fletch's mind. He didn't want to question it and instead decided to enjoy their connection. Compared with his younger years in Seattle, where all his needs were ignored, this visit was noticeably different in so many ways. Fletch had become strong mentally and physically, and knowing his team and Elias had his back, he felt energized even though they were fighting the clock.

Shaw was busy on the phone with Brick, hoping for good news on their end. Hell, any news would be something more than what they had. Even though a few individuals recognized Kyle from one of the pictures, they'd denied it. What the hell was going on around here?

Fletch had made sure to stress he was Kyle's brother if anyone was resistant to talking to the police, but it hadn't helped. Now what?

"You're being watched," Elias whispered while nodding his head to the right.

Sure enough, a sixteen- or seventeen-year-old Hispanic kid was standing in the small alley between two buildings staring straight at him. Once they locked onto each other, the stranger motioned with his head to follow him down the alley. Then he was gone.

Fletch stood and headed straight to the alley, trusting Elias to grab Shaw and bring him along. He stopped at the entrance to see the kid had moved down to the other end, and Fletch followed him in. He didn't give a shit where he had to go to get information on his brother's whereabouts.

He could depend on Elias and Shaw to have his back if anything got out of hand, or they were about to be ambushed. When he got closer, the kid continued down a second side street headed east toward the river. Not a word was said, but the kid kept rechecking they were still following him.

The pungent smell of the river was getting stronger until they finally came to an industrial building with a couple of faded marina signs and plywood covering all the windows.

"Not spooky at all," Shaw grumbled from behind him. "Let's follow the unknown bogey into the dark, abandoned building. Seems safe."

Yeah, maybe this was far enough without telling them what he wanted. "We're not going any farther until you tell me what you know." Fletch's training was sending off warning bells.

The kid looked confused and said, "You've come for your brother."

"Yes, I'm here to find Kyle."

"Then you must come with me."

Damn right he would.

"If this is some trap, it won't end well for you," Elias advised in his calm cop no-nonsense manner.

"It isn't a trap, but we must hurry before we're seen," the kid said.

Fletch went on full alert and followed him into the building. There was hardly any light, but he was at home in the dark. So many missions had been conducted in blackout conditions.

They transferred into a building on the other side of the first and were at the end of the second building before he saw the first bits of light shining out from around a closed door. He could hear voices on the other side before the kid knocked on the door, and everyone went silent.

"This isn't fucked-up at all," Fletch said as Elias and Shaw joined him. All were armed, but that was the last thing he wanted to happen. Elias had his Glock out and down by his side, ready for anything.

The doorknob turned, and the door opened a few inches. The kid who led them there leaned in and whispered something to whoever was inside. The door opened, and they were motioned inside.

This was the moment they'd find out if they were suckers.

Fletch crossed the threshold, and whatever he'd imagined was waiting for him, this wasn't it. Two older women and four young women sat on overturned boxes and old pails in a small room lit by a kerosene camping lantern. What did this have to do with his brother?

"Please sit," one of the older women with almost white hair said as she pointed to a two by six piece of lumber that had been made into a makeshift bench.

Fletch looked back at Elias and Shaw, who both nodded, and they all sat. All four girls were Hispanic, while the two older women were Black and Caucasian. The kid didn't enter the room, remaining outside to guard the door.

"Shaw, let Brick and the others know we're okay," Fletch said, knowing full well their leader would've been tracking them by now. The last thing he needed was for the rest of the team to come crashing in guns blazing.

"Done," he replied.

"May we see your identification, Fletcher?" the same woman asked.

"My ID?"

"Yes. We must make sure you are who you say you are."

He could buy that so he dug out his driver's license from his wallet and handed it to her. She took it closer to the light and adjusted her glasses as she read the license. When she appeared satisfied he was who he said he was, she returned it to him. Then she went to the other woman who reached down into a fabric bag sitting on the dusty floor beside her and pulled out the last thing he would have ever guessed.

"A safe?" Fletch said as she brought it over and handed it to him.

It didn't have the keypad of newer models but a dial lock on the front panel. He estimated it was the size of a desk drawer and weighed roughly ten pounds. The more he looked at it, the more he began to realize that he'd seen it before.

"Kyle gave that to us to hide if he didn't come back and we were to wait until his brother came looking for him," the woman who'd remained seated explained.

"When was the last time you saw him?" Elias asked.

"Sixteen days ago," she stated without hesitation.

"Sometime between the last time your parents spoke to him and his assistant reporting him missing," Elias laid out the timeline.

"I'm afraid your parents are lying," she said bluntly.

"There's a big shock," Shaw huffed.

"What do you mean?" Fletch asked the woman.

"Kyle told me he was going over to speak with them after leaving the safe with us, and Maria confirmed she'd seen his car leaving their driveway late the next evening," she explained.

"Maria? Who's Maria?" Elias asked.

The woman looked over to one of the four girls and proceeded to speak to her in Spanish. Fletch had never learned the language, so he was unsure what was said, but the girl's head began nodding up and down.

"Maria worked for the Biedermans up until recently," the seated lady said.

"The house across the street from them," Elias confirmed.

"Yes."

"Why would Kyle leave this safe with you?" Fletch asked, wanting more information. "How did you meet him?"

"Kyle came to us."

"Why?" Fletch asked.

"Because he found me hiding in his parents' backyard." One of the other teenage girls spoke up. "He saved me."

"Let's start from the top," Shaw said.

"Yes. Of course. My name is Laura, and this is my friend, Crystal," the woman said before sitting down in a chair beside Crystal. "We work to help these young girls gain their freedom."

"You mean getting them into the country from Mexico?" Elias asked.

The older women looked at each other before Laura continued, "Not in the way you believe. We save them from the human traffickers who brought them here to work as servants to the rich and reputable of this city."

"Fuck," Shaw groaned. "Are we dealing with some organized crime kingpin or some shit?"

"Worse, the people who make the laws or have the power and money to bend them to their will," Crystal said.

Shit.

***

"Mr. Kyle found Alejandra hiding in the trees behind your parents' house," Laura continued.

"He was putting something away in the garage," Alejandra said.

"Why were you hiding?" Elias asked, not looking forward to the answer. He'd seen some of the worst of society in his lifetime, but human trafficking was by far the worst of organized crime.

"Because Mr. Jules's house backs onto the Daniels' property, and I was trying to stay away from the house until Mr. Jules passed out." The young woman looked down as if she were reliving the moment, making Elias sick to think what she went through. "He was drunk again and angry. You have to hide, or bad things happened."

"Bad things?" Fletch asked.

Laura spoke up for the young woman. "Yes, it's as disgusting as you're imagining. Instead of ignoring her plea for help, Kyle hid her in his car and brought her back to his apartment."

"I swear to this day the Lord had me working that helpline that night," Crystal said. "Kyle had called the Women's Abuse Hotline after Alejandra begged him not to call the police because she was an undocumented immigrant."

"We'd been hearing rumors about a human trafficking ring moving young women up the west coast from a location in Ensenada, Mexico," Laura said. "We work in the shelters and food kitchens, anywhere we see a need, and news travels fast among the homeless."

"Ensenada?" Fletch asked, looking shocked. Elias would have to ask him about that later.

"Yes, but we don't have an exact location," Crystal confirmed. "It's a staging area before the girls are smuggled across the border with dreams of a better life."

"Only to discover when they arrive that they'd been entered into servitude with the threat of violence, being thrown out, and reported to Immigration and Customs Enforcement to keep them in line," Laura explained. "Who would believe an illegal woman over a well-known businessman, or even a judge?"

"Who are the people involved?" Shaw asked.

"We don't know how deep it goes, but Kyle was gathering information. I imagine that's what's in the safe," Laura said. "We noticed a few of the girls have come from Medina and Denny-Blaine communities."

"Are there more girls and women out there?" Elias asked, fearing the worst.

"Yes. Some locked into the residences, and others who've managed to get away don't last long on the streets. We try to catch as many as we can without drawing attention to ourselves," Crystal explained.

"How long has this been going on, and what happens next?" Elias asked.

"Almost five years. We hide them among the Hispanic community and off Immigration's radar. They have nothing to return to in Mexico with threats of violence to themselves and their loved ones if they return."

Fletch was quiet, and Elias squeezed his shoulder in support. "Kyle's disappearance has everything to do with what he'd found out."

"I remember when he bought this safe," Fletch said. "That's what has been bothering me since finding the numbers. He bought it at an antiques shop in Kensington in San Diego on our vacation. I asked him why he didn't wait and buy one in Seattle instead of lugging this thing around in his car."

"What did he say?" Elias asked.

"That there were certain things he wanted to keep safe before he returned home. Why wouldn't he have told me all this?" Fletch asked, and Elias could hear the pain in his voice. "He even read out the combination in front of me. I hadn't been paying attention because I thought it wasn't important."

"I can tell you why he didn't tell you," Crystal said, getting Fletch's attention. "When he came to hide the safe with us and told me to give it to no one other than his brother, I asked him why he wouldn't give it to you himself. Kyle said that your family had already done enough damage to you, and he refused to drag you in unless something happened to him."

Shaw stood and handed Crystal a card. "That is our team's information."

"We can help keep these girls safe and out of anyone's hands, I promise," Fletch swore before standing. "The sooner we get this open, the sooner we find out what the hell is going on and put a stop to it."

"You are so much like your brother. It's plain to see." Laura pulled out a folded piece of paper and handed it to Fletch. "This is how to contact us. We thank you for any bit of help you can provide."

"We'll be in touch. If something happens or if you need help, call us," Elias said before the three of them turned to backtrack their way out.

Elias's commitment to the law stood in stark contrast to what he was doing by not reporting the girls to ICE. However, he chose to look at the larger picture. Individuals used these young women's desperation for the American dream to break the laws they demanded and created. In his mind, the women were innocent pawns, and they deserved a chance at a better future.

"Wait," Crystal said, stopping them in their tracks. "Maybe you should take the bag. It'll look odd for you to be walking around with a drawer safe under your arm."

Elias looked down at the black and silver box. "Right, should have thought of that."

Once they had it covered, they followed the same kid out a completely different way than when they came in. Smart.

When they got to the last of the buildings, the kid pointed toward the street, and they parted ways. When they reached Fourteenth Avenue again, Cooper was surprised to find Brick and the others waiting for them.

"How did they know where we were?" he asked.

"They've been tracking us the moment we stepped into that alley and have been monitoring us ever since," Fletch explained.

Damn, they were as good as he'd heard.

Chapter Twelve

Fletch set the metal safe on the coffee table and carefully turned the dial in the sequence they'd found on the piece of paper hidden behind the picture of him and his brother. Each click thundered through his head until he reached the final number, popping the safe open.

He poured what was inside onto the table. A journal, an envelope filled with pictures, and an external hard drive. Fletch reached for the journal while Spence took the hard drive, and Brick handed out the pictures.

"Let's see if we recognize anybody," Brick said.

Fletch opened the journal to find a note addressed to him.

Hey Fletch,

Since you're reading this, I can only assume the worst has happened, and I'm missing or dead. I'm sorry to lay this all at your feet. I tried to keep you out of harm's way. You now have the safe I'd given Crystal to keep hidden. I had no doubt you would find it.

When I began researching the women's claims, I had no idea how far the human trafficking went. Once I did, I wasn't sure who to trust. I've left you a large paper trail that includes the names of high-ranking members of Seattle society, and all the proof you need to start is here in my notes, pictures, and on my hard drive.

I have one more thing to confirm before going forward to the media with what I've found.

I love you, brother. Don't be too mad I kept this from you. I'll be able to tear up this note with any luck before you must read it.

Kyle

Fletch's hands shook as he handed the note over to Elias, who read it aloud.

"We have to figure out what that last piece of information is," Brick said. "It might lead us to the kidnappers."

"Why would Chuck and Liz say they spoke to him on a different day?" Shaw asked.

"I think I know why," Fletch said, ready to share what had come back to him while they were still in the building with the women. "My parents have a vacation home in Ensenada."

"Where they believe the traffickers meet up before heading across the border," Elias said what Fletch was thinking.

"Yeah." His stomach was churning. *How could they?*

"How are they getting across so successfully?" Spence asked.

"Is this your parents' property?" Roman asked as he raised a photo for Fletch to see.

Sure enough, the bastards were involved. "Yeah. My mom inherited it when Grandma passed away. Grandma liked to escape to the warmer weather."

Now that he had confirmation they were involved, the pieces began falling into place, except his parents never had a maid for as long as he could remember. Of course, that could've changed over the past two decades.

"Maybe he went over to confront them? Get them to turn themselves in or something," Spence suggested.

"That's what Kyle's car was doing there that night," Fletch said. "Giving the bastards a chance to do the right thing."

"Then he disappeared." Brick put a sharp point on it. His parents had to be involved with Kyle's disappearance.

"Guys," Spence said while looking at his screen. "There are some powerful names on this list Kyle saved on this hard drive. I'm talking about a judge, heads of corporations, law enforcement, and even a senator. It's going to take me a day or two to go through it all thoroughly."

"I think a second visit to my parents' home is in order. Only off the radar this time," Fletch suggested. If they were hiding anything, he wanted to know about it.

"What about Detective Sommers? Do we share this with him? How do we know he's not compromised?" Roman asked, thinking of all the angles.

"Ray would never be a part of this," Elias stated. "I've served with him long enough to know the man. He'd sooner take a bullet than harm an innocent."

Fletch could hear the conviction in Elias's voice, and he wanted to believe him, but he knew they'd have to confirm it no matter what.

"I ran his name, and it doesn't appear in Kyle's records," Spence announced. "And he was clean when I checked him out after our first meeting."

"You did a background check on Ray?" Elias asked.

"Hell, I did a background check on you too," Spence confirmed with a grin. "You had a bit of a lead foot when you were younger, Sheriff."

Elias shook his head. "You're thorough. I can respect that, but I can assure you Ray's not involved."

"We'll have to confirm it either way before sharing this information with him. We can't risk tipping the wrong people off until we come up with a plan to get Kyle back and end the human trafficking," Brick stated. "In the meantime, I want everything from the safe to be gone over so that there are no more surprises. We need to get up to speed."

Fletch agreed with Brick, they had to make sure about Ray, but he didn't want to make it seem like he didn't believe Elias. People can hide who they are from even the closest of friends and family. He knew that better than anyone. His parents could be responsible for his brother's disappearance.

On the other hand, he understood how Elias was feeling. He'd feel the same if someone doubted one of his team members.

"We have to make sure, Elias. I hope you understand." He didn't know what else to say.

Elias turned to face him on the couch and ran his hand over Fletch's stubbled jaw. "I understand, and I'd never put anyone here in danger, especially you. You'll see he can be trusted."

"That's what I want as well," Fletch confirmed. "Want to help me go over Kyle's journal?"

"You bet. With any luck, this will lead us straight to Kyle."

"I hope so."

"Me too."

***

As quietly as possible, Elias brushed his teeth in their en suite bathroom so as not to wake Fletch. It was early, and they'd been up most of the night reviewing Kyle's notes, and Elias wanted to allow his man to rest as much as possible. He hadn't bothered turning on the lights, choosing to use the glow of the streetlights outside their rental. The sun hadn't slipped above the horizon yet.

The information Kyle had uncovered was damning to those on the list, but what concerned him were the names not on that list. Who were they, and what position did they hold in this organization? Were other states involved? There were so many layers left to be dug up that no one knew where it would end.

Of course, a cartel was involved even though the kind ladies who protected the trafficked young women thought not. Nothing went down in Mexico without the cartel's say, but the problem was figuring out who they were. Somewhere in Sinaloa was his best guess since Ensenada was in Sinaloa. When dealing with cartels, someone always ends up dead, and he prayed it wasn't Kyle. It would destroy Fletch, and Elias never wanted innocent people to suffer.

He couldn't help but respect Kyle Daniels for what he'd tried to do with this information. The brothers were a lot alike. More than what their parents might wish. Would someone kill their child to protect themselves? They'd soon find out.

"Elias?" Fletch's voice was rough with sleep.

He rinsed the toothpaste from his mouth, wiped off his wet chin, and headed back into the bedroom.

"Hey. I'm right here. All's good. Why don't you try to get some more sleep? It's early."

"Why don't you come back to bed?" Fletch countered.

"I can do that." Damn straight he could.

Elias pulled the sheets back and discovered Fletch was naked. He could've sworn he'd had his boxer briefs on last night. He dove back in without asking and took his *love* into his arms. As that word crossed his mind, Elias had to admit that it was true. He'd fallen in love with this strong, brave, caring, amazing man.

"I love you, Fletcher," he said as he pulled him closer to his side. "You don't have to say anything. I just wanted you to know."

Fletch's head popped up so fast that Elias was forced to lean back to keep him in focus.

"I love you too," Fletch whispered, his voice husky. "I wasn't sure if I should say anything. Hell, most of our time together has been a chaotic mess. I wouldn't have blamed you if you'd run for the hills."

Elias could feel his heartbeat speeding up. "Never be afraid to tell me anything. We're together in this, our team of two, and I have no intention of going anywhere without you."

Fletch's smile widened. "Yeah, our team. I like that." Leaning forward, he took Elias's lips in a deep, passionate kiss that had him moaning with desire.

Their tongues dueled as Elias wrapped his arms around Fletch's chest and slid him over until his man was on top of him. Their mouths never broke apart, and Elias continued his exploration as he ran his hands down Fletch's muscled back until he was cupping his lover's firm, round butt cheeks. His fingers traced down slowly to circle his hole, making Fletch spread his legs even wider.

Their bodies molded together, and Elias could feel Fletch's hard-on pressing against his own. The only problem was Elias still had on his boxer-briefs, or they'd already be skin to skin. He desperately wanted skin to skin: to have nothing between them.

Fletch backed off and sat up on his knees, asking, "Can I remove your underwear?" Elias loved that they were on the same wavelength. Consent was a serious turn-on. To know the person wholly and completely wants the same thing you do.

"Hell yeah," Elias agreed. "I want nothing between us."

Elias watched as his lover's pale, freckled, calloused hands ran down his abdomen and reached for the waistband of his boxer-briefs. He loved the apparent differences between them but knowing inside they were the same: two gay men in love finding their way together.

His cock was straining for release from the piece of cloth restraining it. When Fletch lifted the elastic waistband over his throbbing erection, Elias groaned in pleasure. Soon he was as naked as his lover, who he pulled back into his arms.

The moment they were touching, Fletch began licking his way up the side of Elias's neck, driving him crazy with need. His hips bucked, rubbing their pelvises together while leaving wet trails from their leaking cocks across their abdomens.

Both were busy exploring the other's body as their hands, lips, and tongues took over. Elias wanted to touch and taste his lover, memorizing every moan and gasp. Fletch's hard-muscled body shivered when he took hold of his cock.

"Oh yeah," Fletch moaned.

Elias pumped his hand in time with Fletch's hips as he swallowed his lover's groan in a slow kiss. Without giving his man any warning, Elias flipped them so he was now on top, looking down at his prize.

"I love you," Elias said, allowing his emotions free rein. "Can I make love to you?" He wanted to make sure they were still on the same page considering everything Fletch was going through.

"You top?"

"Yeah." Elias was what he was, but that didn't mean he couldn't try changing up for his lover.

"I haven't bottomed a lot, but can't wait to feel this beast sliding into me," Fletch said while running the palm of his hand up Elias's cock. "Do you have supplies?"

"Does it make me look bad if I said yes?" Elias asked. Considering they were here to find Kyle, sex shouldn't've been on his mind, let alone him packing for it.

"No, it doesn't. It means you're prepared," Fletch said with a sexy grin. "Speaking of preparing, let's get this show on the road." He wiggled his hips to get his point across.

"Yes, sir. On it," Elias said as he jumped out of bed and over to his canvas bag he'd left sitting on the low dresser on the other side of the room.

He'd thrown condoms and lube in at the last minute, and now he was so glad he did. Within seconds he was back in bed, hovering over Fletch. Elias set the condom on the bedside table and took the plastic security seal off the new bottle of lube before popping it open.

"Ready?" he asked, barely able to contain his excitement.

Fletch smiled and spread his legs a bit wider. "Hell yeah."

Between his heated stare and the excited hum of his body, Elias knew Fletch was more than ready for him, and he was happy to oblige.

***

Fletch had to admit he was nervous. He hadn't been lying when he said he didn't bottom often, but with his excitement and need skyrocketing with every move, it didn't last long. The first touch of Elias's lubed finger to his hole sent fire racing through his veins, and he wanted more.

Slowly his lover spread the lube over Fletch's hole before sliding the tip of his index finger inside. At first, it felt odd but soon morphed into a crashing wave of need that had him begging for more.

Time stood still as Elias lavished him with attention. While one hand continued to stretch him, the other roamed over his body, pinching his nipples and causing goosebumps to rise all over Fletch's skin. The man's talented tongue worked its way up from Fletch's abdomen to his neck, allowing the sensations to swamp him as a riptide of desire pulled him under.

By the time Fletch was ready, he was a moaning puddle in the middle of the bed. Elias reached for the condom, but he beat him to it.

"I'd like to put this on you. Is that okay?" Fletch asked. He knew he liked it when someone did that for him.

By the fire in Elias's eyes, he had his answer, but his lover put a voice to his response. "Yesss."

Fletch tore the package open and threw the wrapper onto the bedside table before setting the latex over the mushroomed head of Cooper's hard cock and slowly rolling it down his thick shaft. His lover moaned his approval as Fletch pumped his hand up and down, making the big man's head fall back on his shoulders.

"Damn, your touch is incredible," Elias groaned as Fletch cupped his balls and rolled them in his fingers while still pumping his latex-covered cock.

Fletch finally understood it didn't matter who was in which position. This wasn't about power because he had all the power even though he wasn't currently the top. This was about love, trust, and pleasure as they found their way together. Two strong men sharing their lives and allowing change so they could grow as one.

Elias pulled back and lined the head of his cock up with Fletch's hole. "Ready, love?"

Fletch didn't even have to take a moment to think about it. "Show me what you've got, Marine."

Elias's eyes lit up at the challenge, and he instantly began pushing forward, spreading Fletch wide. Moans were torn from his soul, and he arched his back as Elias filled him. Going from famine to feast took a little bit of time for his body to accommodate the newness of the sensation, but, once Elias began moving and applying more lube, everything fell into place, and they set a furious pace.

Fletch caught Elias's lips in a punishing kiss that had them both gasping when they broke apart. His skin felt electrified as their two bodies became one in a haze of need. He lost track of time as everything faded away, leaving the two of them alone in their small world.

"You feel so good," Elias growled, angling his hips until he brushed Fletch's prostate on every thrust. "There it is."

"Fuck yeah," Fletch hissed while taking hold of his cock and pumping it along with Elias's hips. "That's it, don't stop." His orgasm was riding him hard, and he was about to blow. "I'm going to come." Electricity shot up his spine, out to every point of his body before racing back down into his throbbing balls.

Elias redoubled his efforts until all Fletch could do was throw his head back and roar his release to the ceiling as wave after wave of pleasure washed over him. Somewhere in his endorphin-filled brain, he heard Elias follow him over the same cliff.

His man lowered his body to blanket Fletch. Their kisses were languid and relaxed, and he could barely keep his eyes open.

"Rest, love," Elias crooned. "I'll clean us up."

Fletch barely noticed the bed shift when Elias got up. Sleep was closing in fast. He hadn't been getting decent sleep for days, and it seemed as if all the exhaustion was coming to crash down on him at this moment.

The next thing he knew, Elias was covering him with the blankets and pulling him close.

"Love you, Elias," he said as his eyes reclosed.

"Love you too, Fletch."

Chapter Thirteen

There was a knock on the front door, and the team waited for Elias to answer it. Ray had called to say he was on the way over with news, so there was no better time to ask the detective a few questions.

Fletch watched as Ray stepped inside after exchanging a few words with Elias. His smile appeared genuine as he joined them in the living room.

"How did your search in South Park go?" Ray asked as he looked around.

"It was a bust," Brick said. "You have news for us."

"I was worried that would be a dead end, but I have some news," he said before sitting in a chair and opening the file he'd brought. "After the ransack of Kyle's apartment, I decided to go back to square one and had his car dusted for prints. They hadn't done it the first time around because there was no sign of foul play."

"What did you find?" Fletch asked, but he had a feeling he already knew.

"Along with your brother's prints, I found two other persons of interest. Elizabeth Daniels and Judge Wilkens. I contacted your parents' lawyer to ask if she'd ever driven Kyle's car, and I received a response of no, which is an obvious lie as her prints were found on the steering wheel, gear shift, and seat controls. As for Judge Wilkens, I have no idea why a Superior Court judge's fingerprints would be found on the passenger side of Kyle's car. Fletch, do you know if they were acquaintances?"

"He never mentioned the man to me," Fletch said, and he technically wasn't lying. Kyle may not have told him the name, but his notes in the safe did. The judge was dirty as they came.

"Okay, so I'll get them both to come in for questioning," Ray said as he wrote something in his notes. "I'm sorry to say, I believe even stronger now your parents are involved in Kyle's disappearance."

He looked genuinely sorry to have to tell him his parents were dirty.

"You're going to bring Judge Wilkens into the station for formal questioning?" Shaw asked. "On the record?"

"That's how it usually happens in an investigation. The judge has to have a reason for being in Kyle's car, and I want to know what that is." Ray looked around at their group. "Does somebody want to tell me what's going on?"

"First, we'd like to ask you a few questions, Detective Sommers. Is that okay with you?" Brick asked straight out.

Ray didn't hesitate. "You can ask me anything you'd like."

"Who was on this case before Elias called you and asked you to take it over?"

"Detective Roserio was the first person assigned to the case." That was another name on the list that had ties to the cartel.

"How did he behave when you replaced him?" Spence asked.

"He wasn't there to say anything. Roserio's on vacation."

"When is he due back?" Brick asked.

"I don't know. I didn't ask," Ray answered easily.

"What's your read on the detective?" Elias asked.

"I don't know the man personally, but on the job, I find he's lazy and unmotivated," Ray said. "My turn to have a question answered. You did find something in South Park, right?"

"Yeah."

"And whatever it is has you unsure of me or law enforcement in general?"

"Both," Brick answered.

Ray looked over at Elias in question, and Fletch couldn't allow him to doubt his friend. "Elias has been defending you."

Ray nodded his head in understanding. "I don't know what to do to reassure you. It's not like I carry around a lie detector."

"It just so happens," Spence said, "that I have a modified version of a lie detector right here." He pointed over at the shoebox-size device sitting on the side table against the wall.

"If Elias tells me that's a real lie detector that's accurate, I will let you wire me up."

"That's why I had them test it on me first. I would never have a friend do something I wasn't willing to do," Elias said.

"And?"

"It caught me in every lie I tried. As far as I can tell, it works."

"Okay, let's do this," Ray agreed.

Spence stood and walked over to Ray. "I'll have to connect these wires to certain points on your body. It shouldn't take long."

Ray nodded, and Elias sat down beside Fletch. He could feel the stress coming off his man, so Fletch began rubbing circles on Elias's back, hoping to calm him. When Elias's shoulders lowered ever so slightly, he knew it'd been the right move.

A few minutes later, Ray was hooked up to the machine, looking calm. Damn, he hoped the guy passed because he was beginning to like him and it would hurt Elias if he didn't.

"Okay, we can begin," Spence said as he watched the lines appearing on his computer screen. "Let's begin with something easy. Would you please tell me your name?"

"Ray Sommers."

"How long have you worked as a detective?"

"Five years in November."

"This time, I need you to lie. How old are you?" Spence asked.

"Nineteen."

The lines changed noticeably compared to the first two answers.

"Got it. You can start any time, Brick."

Brick moved closer to the coffee table. "Ray, are you or have you ever been involved with a Mexican cartel."

"No."

Spence wrote something down, and Brick continued. "Do you know where Kyle Daniels is located?"

"No."

"Have you ever taken a bribe to look the other way involving criminal activity?"

"No."

"Will you uphold the law no matter what you learn in this case?"

"Yes."

"Looks good to me," Spence said. "We can unhook him."

"Wait, I have a question," Elias interrupted with a grin on his face. "Did you eat the last two chocolate bars I had hidden in my bunk right before we left on that mission to Guatemala?"

Ray broke out into a huge smile. "Who, me?" The lines began to get jagged before Spence removed the wires.

"I knew it. No one else had the balls to do it," Elias huffed.

"They were good too," the detective said with a grin.

"You couldn't have left me one?"

"Okay, okay. Let's get on with this," Brick said. "You're right. We received information that has a list of people involved in a human trafficking ring here in Seattle."

Ray's face went pale. "Human trafficking? Fuck, and the judge is on that list?"

"Yeah," Fletch spoke up. "My brother had the evidence to take them down before he went missing."

"They found out?" Ray asked.

"We believe he went over to his parents' home to give them the chance to turn themselves in and work with the police," Brick explained.

"Someone confirmed they saw his car in their driveway," Shaw added.

"Do you think they turned on him and called in the judge?" Ray asked, and it appeared the picture was coalescing for the detective. "That's why his fingerprints are in Kyle's car. Elizabeth must have driven it back to his apartment to park it like nothing ever happened."

"I'm afraid Detective Roserio is on that list as well," Elias said.

"No wonder you were suspicious of me. Hell, I would be in your shoes. Is there any chance I can see this list?" Ray asked.

Everyone turned to Fletch. It was his brother's life on the line. "We'll share what we have, but it stays between us for now. I have to find Kyle first before they cut their losses and disappear."

"I'm truly sorry, Fletch. You don't deserve to have to go through what you have," Ray said. "But I swear I won't stop until we find him."

"Thank you," Fletch said. "I'll never quit." It was the motto for the Navy SEALs and how he chose to live his life.

"All in, all the time," Brick stated.

"Hooyah," the team cheered.

***

"The street's clear," Spence's voice said over his tactical headset, allowing them to whisper and still be heard. Spence said it had something to do with bone hearing technology, and Elias had to admit he could hear everyone no matter how low or far away.

They'd been running surveillance on the parents' house for hours, and there was nothing new to report. It was midnight, and their team was scattered throughout the community, keeping watch. Since Ray had contacted Elizabeth about driving Kyle's car, there'd been an uptick in action around the house.

Cars came and went, and the team cataloged every license plate and photographed every person. However, the Danielses barely left their home, making it difficult to have a good look around the property, which was necessary to push forward in the investigation.

Ray was off meeting with a CI who said he had information on a debt that would be of interest to them.

"Wait, I see movement out back," Shaw said.

"What is it?" Fletch asked.

"Looks like Charles and Elizabeth are on the move. They came out the back door and are getting into their Bentley," Shaw confirmed.

Elias watched from his perch from among the skids of lumber on a lot for a new house three streets over. The Danielses didn't bother turning on their headlights as they drove down their lane before turning right, heading north.

"I'll follow them," Shaw said.

"I'll go have a look around inside," Fletch stated.

"Give me a minute to override their security system," Spence told him, and Elias watched as their new rental car went past the house in the same direction as the Danielses.

They'd decided to rent an additional vehicle Fletch's parents hadn't seen. With any luck, the midsize four-door would go unnoticed.

"Okay, I've got control of the security system. You can move in," Spence stated.

Elias didn't move. His job was to remain outside and act as a lookout in case the Danielses returned. He watched through his specially designed binoculars that worked with little or no light as Fletch and Brick breached the property through the stand of trees then headed straight for the back of the house.

"Be careful," Elias couldn't help saying even though he knew full well Fletch could take care of himself.

"Love you too," Fletch said before disappearing from sight. This was going to be the longest few minutes of his life.

Chapter Fourteen

Fletch hugged the tree line for as long as he could before making his break for the back of his parents' house. He unscrewed the bulb from the sidelight when they reached the back door, blanketing them in darkness.

He stood watch as Brick moved in to pick the lock. The night was quiet with only the moon as their witness. The weather in Seattle would be turning cold soon. He couldn't help but wonder if Kyle was somewhere warm. Moments later, they were inside. The previous feeling of being watched wasn't there this time around as they moved from the back laundry room into the house.

Some of the finishing may have changed, but the old layout remained, providing Fletch with the ability to move quickly from room to room. Brick followed him through the kitchen and into his father's study, which was eerily the same as he remembered. Dark paneling covered the walls while highly polished hardwood flooring shone in the moonlight coming in through the windows.

He'd received an uncountable number of lectures in this room throughout his childhood. Spent mostly with his head down, watching his reflection in the hardwood. Two of the walls held custom floor-to-ceiling bookcases typically packed full of books, but not now. There was barely enough to cover one shelf.

"Where did all the books go?" Fletch mused aloud. "This room had been full the last time I saw it."

Then he saw the monitors set up along the back wall. "So that's why we felt like someone was watching us because someone was. We need to find out who that person was."

"I'll search the desk," Brick said. "I want you to get a better look around the house overall. I'm curious what else is missing."

"Same here," Fletch agreed. "The place looks bare."

He turned and went back out the study door and continued past the living room he'd seen at their first meeting and to the stairs.

Slowly, he ascended to the second story, watching ahead for any movement. Sure, they believed his parents were here alone, but you could never be too careful. It wasn't as if they'd tell them.

When he reached the landing, once a communal space at the top of the stairs, Fletch found it empty. His mother's Bosendorfer grand piano, which had sat front and center, taking advantage of the lofty ceilings and large space, was nowhere in sight. She'd played it every day when he was young. Now, there wasn't even a plant in this room, making it an eerily dead space.

Down the hall were five closed doors, the bedrooms, and the bathroom. He came to the first door, which used to be his and Kyle's bedroom, and opened it. Empty. Another empty room. It wasn't as if he thought his parents would keep anything of his as a memento of their firstborn son, but Kyle had been wiped out as well.

He shut the door to ensure he left no trace they were there. He came to the bathroom, which looked unused and ready for an update with its green toilet and tub, then to his sisters' room, finding it much the same condition as the other. It seemed even the golden daughters didn't survive the purge.

The spare bedrooms were barren, as well as having a thick layer of dust covering everything. It appeared that no one had been in them for years. When Fletch came to the end of the hallway, the only room left to check was his parents' master bedroom. To say this was creepy as fuck was an understatement, but he pushed on.

He opened the door and could barely see inside because the curtains had been drawn, covering all the windows. Fletch took out his pencil light, knowing no one would be able to see the glow outside, and stepped into the one place he'd never been allowed.

This room had some furniture, a queen bed, a couple of high-backed lounge chairs near the bay window, and a small coffee table set between. It was clean and tidy but nowhere near his parents' preference for excess. The vanity area in their en suite bathroom was devoid of fancy perfume bottles, cologne, creams in their gold jars, and those Mason Pearson hairbrushes his mother liked. He never understood the need for brushes costing hundreds of dollars. What was left there appeared old and well used. There was nothing new.

Elizabeth Daniels was known to go on shopping sprees for no reason. Coming home with designer dresses and handbags she'd wear to lectures to appear "more" than the other professors and drawing that line in concrete. The message was clear: The Danielses were better than all of them. Fletch wasn't making that up in his imagination. He'd heard his mother talking about how far above she was than the head of her department at the university. She referred to the other woman as a simpleton wasting her money on books and charities.

He moved on to their walk-in closet only to find more of the same, and there wasn't a designer bag in sight. Half the racks were empty and what was left looked like a hodgepodge of pieces taken from what their wardrobe used to be. There was no question in his mind: his parents were in financial straits. They'd been liquidating their belongings for a while, but why? They still had their high-paying jobs, not to mention all the money they'd inherited.

There should have been more than enough to keep them living comfortably for the rest of their lives. Where did it all go?

On top of the dresser sat a stapled stack of paper. Carefully, he used a nearby pen to lift the pages to read what was inside. It was a residential sales agreement for the house in Ensenada between his parents and Salvador Realty. Spence had already checked, and his parents were still listed as owners of the house in Mexico. Were they planning to sell it at one point? And why hadn't they?

Fletch continued through the bedroom, using his flashlight to scan each area before moving on to the next. He noticed discoloration on the walls indicating where a painting had been hung and removed.

At the foot of their bed, the Persian rug was worn almost bare along with the silk comforter on the bed. When he moved on to the chairs, his light caught something darker on the pale fabric arm of one chair. As he got closer, Fletch recognized what he was seeing.

Blood.

"I've got blood upstairs in the master bedroom," Fletch announced, his voice cold but his heart pumping double time.

"On my way," Brick replied.

Fletch knelt to get a better look at the stain on the underside of the armrest, and it appeared to be an outline that reminded him of fingers. As if someone had blood on their hand when they sat down in the chair. It was on the right side of the chair, leading him to believe it was from someone's right hand, and by the size of the fingers, the person was a man. His father.

"Whatcha got?" Brick asked as he entered the room.

"Bloody fingerprints under the armrest of that chair," Fletch said as he pointed at the telltale piece of furniture.

"I'll take a sample of it and see if we can find a match," Brick stated before taking a small clear tube from his pocket.

Fletch held the flashlight as Brick opened the lid and pulled out a cotton swab, adding a few drops of liquid to the end before rubbing it over the dried bloodstain. The swab came back red, and Brick dropped it back into the tube.

"Let's pull back before our luck runs out," Brick suggested, and Fletch had to agree they'd been in here long enough. His skin was beginning to crawl.

"Let's go."

Chapter Fifteen

Spence had been gone for over five hours. He'd gone to visit a friend who could run the bloodwork for him but chose not to say who it was. Their communication specialist dealt with a wide range of individuals, and some didn't like their names being thrown around. They didn't question Spence's methods, and he was more than fine with not sharing.

Fletch had been pacing and watching the clock ever since they handed off the sample to Spence. Even if it was only eight in the morning, he was exhausted but refused to rest. He had to find his brother, and he had "hair on the back of his neck standing up" kind of worry time was running out for Kyle.

When Shaw had returned from following Charles and Elizabeth on their late-night drive, they had a new address of interest. His parents had driven to Mercer Island and visited a lakefront cottage a bit off the beaten path. They'd stayed for over two hours before heading back home. They'd made no stops on the way there or back.

While the others prepared for tonight's mission, here he stood praying it wasn't his brother's blood on that chair. His mind was consumed with that one question, and the team had left him alone to work it through.

He watched as Ray parked his unmarked cruiser in the driveway. Fletch had to wonder what the detective's CI had told him and only hoped it helped in their investigation. The knock on the door came soon after, and he went to join the team in the living room.

Elias came to his side and Fletch couldn't help but lean his weight against his man. He was physically and emotionally drained.

"You need to get some rest at some point today if you're going to be ready for tonight," Elias said.

Fletch looked up at his man. "I'll give it a shot after Spence returns with news."

"Even if the blood is your brother's, it doesn't mean worst-case scenario," Elias reasoned. "There's a chance we'll find him at this cottage tonight."

Fletch wanted to be as hopeful, but something about that bloodstain had him spooked. It wasn't the sight of blood itself. God knew, he'd seen his fair share of blood in the service, but it was who the owner was that was driving him crazy.

"What did you find out?" Fletch asked the moment Ray entered the room.

Ray didn't bother sitting down. "This particular CI runs between the illegal gambling houses across the city."

"I think I should sit down for this one," Fletch said. The combination of little to no rest and stress was taking its toll, and he figured one more thing might take him to the edge.

This wasn't the usual way he handled these types of situations, but he was hunting for his brother. This wasn't a mission. This wasn't an assignment. This was his brother. The only blood member of his family who'd stood by him from when they were kids.

His emotions were getting the better of him, and while he knew it, he couldn't stop them from taking over his psyche.

Elias and Shaw joined him, leaving Brick and Ray standing. Roman had to return to Dallas yesterday for meetings within his company, and he had been reluctant to leave Fletch and the team behind.

"He's aware of your family, specifically, your father. From what he witnessed, Charles Daniels had run up debts with every bookie in the city playing the horses, and they wanted their money back."

"That's why there's nothing left of value in the house. They'd sold them off to pay his gambling debts." Made sense. Now he knew where all the money went, but how did that help them find Kyle?

"Unfortunately, it wasn't nearly enough, and the sharks were closing in fast. Then one day, his entire debt was erased," Ray explained, shaking his head.

"Erased? Erased by who?" Shaw asked.

"The cartel," Fletch answered, putting two and two together. "Now they work for them."

"Fuck," Shaw groaned as he ran his hand over his face.

"We've taken on worse," Brick reminded Shaw.

"Salvador Realty." The name was out of Fletch's mouth as quickly as he'd thought of it.

"What?" Elias asked.

"I found a sales agreement for the Mexican house upstairs in my parents' bedroom when I was searching. But Spence said the house was still in my parents' names."

"If they were going to sell, how did the cartel end up using the property with your parents' names still on the ownership?" Ray mused.

"We need to check out this Salvador Realty," Elias told the group.

"Agreed," Brick said.

"If they were trying to sell the house to get money to pay off Charles's gambling debt and the cartel found out about it, leaving it in the two respected American professors' names would be a good front," Elias suggested.

"Do you think this Salvador Realty has something to do with alerting them to the opportunity?" Shaw asked.

"Yeah," Fletch answered.

"Okay, this is what we know. Kyle discovered your parents were involved in trafficking these young women and offered them a chance to turn themselves in before going public. Then he goes missing," Ray summarized.

"Charles's gambling got them in serious debt with the wrong people. When they tried to sell the last thing of worth they owned, the Ensenada house, the cartel was informed by this realtor," Elias continued his take on the scenario.

"They bought up all of Charles's remaining debt and then approached him with a deal he couldn't refuse," Brick joined in.

"And once they were in, there was no way out," Fletch stated.

"Would they turn on Kyle to save their own skins?" Ray asked in what sounded like disbelief.

"Absolutely," Fletch answered. "If it was a choice between him and them, there's no way they'd sacrifice themselves."

"This might get ugly," Shaw groaned.

"It hasn't already?" Elias asked.

"What don't we know, other than Kyle's exact location?" Brick asked.

The front door unlocked, and Spence walked in carrying a large plastic tub. *What could that be for?*

"You don't know that both Kyle's and Charles's DNA were in that sample you took from that chair," Spence said as he dropped the tub with a loud thud. "I've got two more of these out in the SUV."

"First, how the hell did you manage to run the sample that fast? And what the hell is in those tubs?" Ray asked.

"I've got friends in all kinds of places," Spence replied.

"And the tubs?"

"Same."

"My brother's blood was on my father's hand when he sat down in that chair." Fletch's voice came out rough with emotion. He'd make them all pay.

"It was only a small sample. It doesn't mean worst-case scenario. Kyle is still out there for us to find," Brick said, much the same as Elias had. The thing was, Fletch knew Brick didn't believe in false hope. They'd been in enough tight spots over the years to know if Brick saw shit going sideways, he called it like he saw it. And if he believed their asset was compromised or dead, he said so straight up. Fletch didn't believe Brick was painting a rosy picture for Fletch's benefit, and feeling that in his bones gave him strength.

"Exactly what I was thinking, hence the supplies for mission number two. Considering the cottage we're going to be visiting tonight is out of the way and lakefront, I thought we SEALs could do what we do best and use Lake Washington to our advantage."

Everyone turned to look at Fletch, his mind still whirling, knowing Charles had harmed Kyle in some way.

"What do you think, Fletch?" Elias asked.

His mind became silent, and his fear for his brother's safety morphed into a wave of anger so deep it burned for release.

He stood and looked at his friends. "They'd better pray I find Kyle safe, or I will spend my life tracking down every single one of them."

"We're in this together," Elias confirmed.

The team stood and yelled in unison, "Hooyah."

***

Elias lay silent beside Fletch. He was finally able to convince him resting for a few hours wouldn't affect the raid they'd planned for later tonight. It would give him a chance to recharge and be better prepared.

His lover's head was lying on his chest, and Elias was busy rubbing soothing circles along Fletch's back to help him sleep. Thankfully, it wasn't long before he heard snoring, and he took the opportunity to relax.

The plans for tonight didn't sit well with him. The four-man SEAL team would be coming in on Lake Washington while he and Ray, being law enforcement, would badge up and wait until the cottage was cleared before going in and making arrests. Things needed to be done a certain way to remain on this side of legal.

Spence would be jamming any communication going in and out of the cottage, ensuring that the wrong people wouldn't get the heads-up before they finished. The unknowns were rife with this plan. Would Kyle be there? How many people were in the cottage? What if this location led to another dead end? Fletch would be crushed if his brother wasn't in the cottage, but it was the best lead they had.

Fletch had been right when he'd said their relationship had been surrounded by one craziness after another. However, they'd grown closer with every twist and turn instead of apart. He figured their relationship had the best chance of lasting, considering the adversity they'd encountered and somehow had worked through.

Elias thought about his own family. He hadn't been lying when he said he had an uncle in prison, along with a couple of distant cousins. Most of the rest were gone, and the remaining folks chose to have nothing to do with a lawman. His parents both passed away years ago from cancer, removing the glue from their family. His brother had followed in his footsteps, joining the Marines, and had decided to become a lifer and was now a trainer in the Corp..

Fletch had been so fed up with his biological family that he created his own, only choosing to remain close to Kyle. After hearing stories and meeting good ol' mom and dad, Elias could understand why.

At least he had his parents' love, something Fletch had been denied. Only to discover years later his mother and father were the true criminals in the family as they always stated Fletch would become.

"Kyle..." Fletch moaned, and Elias pulled him closer while continuing to rub his back. His lover wasn't free even in his sleep. All the chaos surrounding them seeped in everywhere.

Back home, Marie had reported all was well in Marshall, and he'd be forever grateful for her and his deputies for holding down the fort while he was gone. She also reported that there'd still been no sign of Frank Edwards anywhere in the county. The longer it took to find the man who'd shot Fletch, the higher his stress level became. Where could Frank be hiding?

Elias lightly brushed his fingers over the healing scar on Fletch's left arm. Evidence of how close he came to losing his man. He knew tonight would be different. This kind of mission was what Fletch had been trained for. He was a specialist, and Elias would have to take a step back, even though he was a Marine, which was hard for him to do.

He was used to taking charge of a situation, leading from the front, and fighting side by side with his men. Waiting on the sidelines was foreign to him, but if he wanted this relationship to work, he had to accept he wouldn't be in the lead all the time. Fletch had integrity, was strong and capable, intelligent and street savvy. Everything Elias wanted.

His former relationships had tended toward noticeable size differences and dominance. He always found himself in the position of protector and top in the past. That fact had been blown out of the water by his amazing man who could protect himself quite handily, along with saving others along the way. It was new, exciting, and much more of a turn-on than he'd expected.

Damn. Everything in his world was changing. Sometimes he found himself confused and worried, but all he had to do was hold Fletch in his arms, and those emotions drifted away.

This was his new life, and if Fletch was in it, Elias had no problem changing his ways. People grew throughout their lives, and this was his opportunity to do it spectacularly. There was no way in hell he'd pass up this opportunity.

As far as he was concerned, they were in this long term, and he wouldn't have it any other way.

Chapter Sixteen

Fletch stretched out his arms in his wet suit, trying to loosen the damn thing considering it was one size too small, but what could he expect with last-minute supplies. His MK 25 rebreather was the main piece of equipment anyway, along with his M4A1. The rebreather allowed them to approach the location from underwater without leaving a trail of bubbles, which would give them away. He adjusted his diving mask and began putting on his fins as did the other three members of his team.

Ray had rented a small boat earlier in the day to get close to the cottage area before they tied it off on a tree and entered the water. They would never leave a boat drifting in the dark, endangering other boaters even though it was late.

They waited in the darkness for confirmation that Ray and Elias were in place. They'd gone over their plan. They were three hundred meters from the cottage and were preparing to get wet.

"We try to confirm Kyle is in the cottage before we enter," Brick said. "Once we have visual confirmation, the rest of us will breach the building farthest away from where Kyle is being held to lead the thugs in the other direction while Fletch heads straight for his brother."

Fletch rechecked his weapons. No one and nothing would come between him and Kyle.

"We need them alive. Dead men can't answer questions," Spence reminded them all.

"That all depends on them," Fletch responded. "If they get in my way or try to harm Kyle, all bets are off."

Spence nodded. The objective of this mission was to save Kyle—if he was in the cottage. Watching all those people on the list pay for what they'd done would come after. He'd love to be there when they handcuffed his parents.

"In place," Elias's voice came over their earpieces. "Two cars in the driveway."

"Time to move," Brick stated. "Let's go get your brother."

Fletch nodded before pulling on his mask and placing the mouthpiece to the rebreather in his mouth. The moment his fins hit the water, he felt at home. He'd spent half his military career in water of some kind or another. This was where he felt comfortable. Where everything made sense and all effort was directed. He'd always felt he was meant to be a Navy SEAL.

The four of them slipped by several houses unnoticed until they were outside the cottage in question. They broke the water's surface with only a small portion of their camouflaged face to get a better look around without coming out of the lake.

There were lights on in two rooms of the cottage. One brighter than the other on either end of the building. They scanned the area, and all was silent, so they removed their fins, threw them over their right arms, and slowly emerged from the water, weapons raised and at the ready.

As a unit, they spread out to different points of the house to have a look inside. Every step was choreographed and measured. As Fletch neared the far right side of the building, he saw movement behind the sheer curtains. Immediately he pressed his back against the building and froze out of sight.

He waited a few seconds before slowly leaning to his left to peek into the window. There was a television on in the room, and it was blaring out contestants' names on some game show. Fletch adjusted his angle and used the mirror reflection of his knife to look to the other side of the room. There he found a man and a woman making out on the couch. Neither would've heard a bomb going off in their current state of undress.

Fletch turned and made it back to their rendezvous site, hoping the others came up with better news.

"I've got one male and one female in the living room getting it on," he announced through his headset.

"Empty spare bedroom," Spence said.

Then Shaw's excited voice gave Fletch what he needed. "I have a figure in what looks like a storage room tied to a chair. I can't see his face. His head is down."

Fletch headed straight to that location. When he found Shaw, instead of talking Fletch went ahead and looked through the window, and sure enough, a male figure sat tied to an old wooden desk chair. There was only a small light off to the side to go by, and the shadows weren't helping.

It had to be Kyle. Who else would be tied up out here? To know his parents came here, allowing this to happen to their son, maybe even participating... Fletch couldn't dwell on it or the red film over his eyes would cloud his brain. But they would pay. He'd make certain they sure as fuck would pay.

"Spence, I need you to cut power to the cottage while Shaw and I go through the front door and straight for the living room. Fletch, you go straight to the person tied up while Spence covers you."

"It's Kyle," Fletch corrected. It had to be.

"I hope so, buddy. I really do," Brick said.

The team split up, and he waited by the window to the spare room. As soon as the power went out, he'd be through that window in seconds, cutting the ropes away from his brother. Nothing else mattered than getting Kyle to safety.

"Three, two," Spence counted down. "One."

The lights went out. Fletch broke the glass out of the windowpane, dove into the room, landing on his feet, and scanning the area. He could hear yelling and screaming coming from the other side of the house.

Quickly, he went to the still figure and clicked on his flashlight, and went about cutting the ropes from his feet, legs, and arms before rounding to the front.

His brother's blue eyes stared up at him through swollen lids, his lip was split, and his face was heavily bruised.

"I knew you'd find me." Kyle's voice came out rough, but his smile was genuine. "I just had to hold on."

"Nothing could stop me," Fletch said as he pulled his brother into his arms.

"I'll call in Elias and Ray and get them to send an ambulance," Spence said from behind him.

"Thanks, man," Fletch said. "Can you stand, Kyle?"

"I'm not sure."

"I've got you," Fletch said as he reached down and lifted Kyle into his arms. "Let's get you out of here."

"I'd like that," Kyle huffed as he laid his head on Fletch's shoulder. He was so light in his arms Fletch was worried they'd starved him, and his legs didn't feel right. Those muthafuckas weren't going to get away with this.

As he cleared the cottage, he could see Elias running in his direction with a first aid kit in his arms. He'd never seen a better sight in his life.

"How bad is he hurt?" Elias asked as he began assessing Kyle's wounds.

Fletch laid his brother down on the decking so that they could get a better look at him. "Where does it hurt the most, bro?"

"My legs are on fire, Fletch," Kyle said as he tried to reach for them.

"Easy, you lie still, and we'll take a look," Elias said as he gently pushed him down. "An ambulance is on the way."

"Are you a doctor?" Kyle asked, looking hopeful.

"I'm a Marine and a sheriff, so don't you worry, we'll get you patched up in no time," Elias answered before lifting Kyle's pantlegs.

Fletch had tight control over his emotions as swift and deadly rage ran through him at the sight of his brother's legs. They were black with bruising, covered in deep rope burns, and his ankles were so swollen his feet were purple.

"You have to stop them, Fletch," Kyle moaned as Elias placed dressings on his legs to stop the bleeding. "I've got proof."

"I have your safe, brother. No one is getting away with anything, especially not our parents." There was no way to keep the growl out of his voice.

Fletch could hear sirens getting closer to their location and knew they only had moments left before chaos ensued.

"You will be guarded at the hospital. No one will get near you again, I swear it."

"He isn't the man I thought he was. They wanted my safe."

"Our father?"

"Yeah," Kyle said, his eyes full of pain. "I should've known better after what they did to you."

"No. None of this is your fault." There was no way in hell he'd let Kyle blame himself. "The people responsible will pay heavily once we get done with them. You have to concentrate on healing."

Kyle's eyelids slid closed and Fletch looked over at Elias, dipped his chin at his brother's legs, and waited.

Elias shook his head. It was as bad as it looked now that he'd cut Kyle's jeans away. He had bruises all over his body. However, his captors chose to exact the most painful damage to his legs.

Elias reached over and cupped the side of Fletch's face. "He's alive and will heal."

Fletch reached for Elias's hand and held on tight. "Yeah, he is."

And that was all that mattered.

Chapter Seventeen

Elias pulled their rental into the driveway of Charles and Elizabeth's Tudor mansion. The curtains were about to be pulled back for all to see how rotten certain high society darlings truly were. Cruisers were fanning out in front and behind him. Some carried on down the street to addresses in the community, while forces blanketed the city for the rest. The list had been specific. No one was being left out of this sweep.

However, all he cared about was the man sitting in the passenger seat beside him. Fletch had been quiet since leaving his brother at the hospital. Brick, Shaw, and Spence were watching over Kyle while they followed Detective Ray to settle some unfinished business.

The doctors were still cataloging Kyle's injuries when they left, but he was in no danger of dying. That was the biggest takeaway from all the information being thrown at Fletch, and Elias was sure that's what his lover was clinging to after seeing what they'd done to Kyle's legs.

Both had been broken in multiple places, along with several fractures in his ankles and feet. They'd made sure if Kyle had somehow gotten free, he wouldn't have been able to run away. The bastards had then tied his legs together as tightly as possible and left him in that damn chair. The rope burns had cut to his bones, and infection had started to set in.

Their father had even used his two hands to administer some of the beatings. As it turns out, when Kyle had gone to his parents' house that night before he disappeared, he never left. At first, Charles and Elizabeth had him tied up in the house, trying to get the location of the information out of Kyle. That's the likely cause of the blood Fletch had found on the armrest.

Kyle couldn't remember being moved to the cottage and was likely unconscious when that occurred. According to his family doctor's health records, he'd lost over thirty pounds and suffered from dehydration.

Fletch's brother had paid a horrible price for trying to do the right thing. Now, they would make sure the bastards who'd caused him so much pain paid handsomely.

Ray and a second police cruiser pulled to a stop outside the house, and Elias pulled up behind them. He placed the SUV in park and turned off the ignition before turning to face Fletch.

"Are you sure you want to be here for this?" He had to make sure. This whole situation was extreme.

"For every second," Fletch stated as he watched one of the officers going around back to make sure his parents didn't try to escape. "This is their day of reckoning."

Fletch opened his door and jumped out, looking like a man on a mission, and Elias was quick to follow.

Side by side, no matter what happened.

They were a team, and he'd be there until his dying day.

***

Fletch could feel an uneasy calm come over him the nearer he got to the front door. When Ray pounded on the thick wood, the sound vibrated through his body. This was the day his parents were knocked off their sanctimonious perch, and he wanted to be there for the fall. He didn't know if that made him a bad person, and right now, he didn't care.

He could hear the locks being opened, and with every click, his heart raced faster. When the door finally opened, it was only by a crack as his mother peered out from behind one of the chain locks.

"We told you to go through our lawyer," Elizabeth sneered. "If you don't leave now, I'll have all of you arrested for trespassing."

"Mrs. Elizabeth Daniels, it's you who is being placed under arrest," Ray announced. "Open the door."

"No, this can't be right," she cried. "I want to speak to my lawyer."

"You're going to want to step back," Fletch warned as he prepared to kick the door open. "Or stay. Either way, this door is coming down."

"What?" Elizabeth's face paled. "You wouldn't dare."

Fletch grinned, "Oh yes the fuck I would." He stepped back and let his steel-toed boot fly.

The door crashed open, and Ray and the other officers stormed in, leaving Elias and Fletch standing outside while his mother was cuffed.

"You'll pay for that," Elizabeth threatened.

Fletch walked in, the glass from the broken sidelight crunching under their feet. "It'll be you who's paying." He walked over and stood directly in front of her. The woman who'd given him life only to turn that life into a living hell until he'd managed to get away when he didn't live up to her exacting expectations. Well, today was payday. "We found Kyle."

Her eyes widened, and her mouth fell open.

"Surprise, mommy dearest. I told you I'd find him," Fletch growled, unable to control his anger, thinking about the shape they'd found Kyle in. "The information you've been trying to beat out of him is now in the hands of law enforcement officials. The ones not on the take. It's over for you and your friends. Don't worry, though. I'm sure you'll make new friends with the other women in prison, many of whom have been victims of human trafficking. Your standing and reputation will mean nothing. In fact, it might attract even more attention, but it won't be the kind you want. You disgust me, and I will see you pay for everything you did to those women, and to Kyle. Your son, you heartless bitch."

Fletch knew the victims of these crimes all too often ended up on the streets desperate to survive any way they could, even having to break the law. While people like Elizabeth sat in their large houses complaining about how the gardener trimmed her rose bush. No lie, the gardener never worked around the community again.

"There's no one else here," an officer reported as he walked into the living room. "We've searched everywhere, and no one went out the back."

"Where is your husband, Elizabeth?" Ray asked.

She looked confused but answered anyway. "He received a call early this morning and had to leave. I don't know when he'll be back."

Fletch couldn't help the laugh the broke free. "The bastard left you here to take the blame while he got away. He got a call warning him, and instead of telling you, he left you here to rot. Fitting for a rat trying to scurry off a sinking ship. There's no loyalty between criminals these days, Ma."

His mother's face filled with rage, but she said nothing. Her eyes narrowed, no doubt weighing her options. He figured it wouldn't be long before she rolled over on her codefendants for a lesser sentence.

"Don't worry. We're rounding up the rest of your group so that you won't be alone for long," Fletch said.

"Let's get you booked. You won't have to call your lawyer. He'll be in a cell alongside you," Ray said, and Fletch didn't miss the grin on his face.

The detective led Elizabeth out the door to the waiting cruiser while he and Elias went to his father's study.

Elias had been silent throughout the confrontation, giving Fletch his quiet support when he needed it. He felt his world was shattering apart at times, but it never lasted long with his partner around. Kyle was alive, he would heal, and while he did, he and the team would be there to help him.

"Is this your father's study?" Elias asked as they walked through the doors. "Holy shit, he liked wood."

"Yeah," Fletch answered. "He loved to lock himself in here away from the rest of us."

"He may be on the run for now, but he won't last long. Either the police will find him or the cartel. He better hope it's us," Elias said as he stared at the paneling to one side of his father's desk.

"What is it?" Fletch could feel Elias's confusion.

"They don't match," he said.

"What doesn't match?" Fletch asked as Ray joined them in the room.

"Elizabeth is off to booking and jail," Ray said. "What's going on?"

"The paneling doesn't match, and its grain is going the opposite direction," Elias said as he walked over behind the desk. "You see here?" Fletch looked closely at the four-foot by two-foot panel. "And compared to this one." Elias pointed to the panel beside it.

The match was close but not exact, as well as the position was off. The wood grain was slightly larger than all the other panels in the room. "There's got to be something behind it."

Fletch took out his pocketknife and began prying the panel off the wall. When he got a quarter of the way down, he stopped, pulled out his flashlight, and looked inside.

"What the hell do we have here?" Fletch asked as he tilted the light to get a better look. "I think they're cassette and videotapes." He stood back and let the other two have a look inside.

"Damn, there have to be dozens of them," Elias said. "Let's get this open and see what we've got."

Fletch went ahead and continued to pry the paneling until there was enough exposed that he could rip the rest from the wall. A cascade of VHS, audio cassettes, Hi8 videotapes, recordable DVDs, and flash drives poured from their hiding spot in the wall. He was positive his father had an easier way to access the hiding spot, but his way had also been effective.

Elias reached down and picked up one VHS videotape and read what was written on the front label. "Salvador 2010."

"The real estate agent," Fletch stated.

"He's being brought in for questioning," Ray said.

"Maybe you guys should have a look at these before questioning him," Elias suggested.

"We will," Ray agreed before calling in one of the officers to collect the evidence.

Fletch was tired, and he wanted to return to his brother. "I'd like to go back to the hospital now."

Elias reached out and took hold of his hand. "I'll take you anywhere you need to go."

"Thanks," Fletch said while pulling Elias closer. "And I mean for everything you've done since the beginning of this mess."

He honestly didn't know how things would have turned out without Elias. Bringing in Detective Ray Sommers, an old friend and an honest cop, to take over the case had been crucial. As it turned out, the previous detective was dirty and on the cartel's payroll.

Elias's quiet strength and support were invaluable after days filled with stress and fear for Fletch's brother to the many sleepless nights. His man had been invaluable. As for the case, he'd provided insights all along the way and noticed the difference in the paneling. Who knows what they would find on those tapes?

"This is the beginning of our story, Fletch, and there's no place I'd rather be."

"The next few months are going to be critical. We need to get Kyle back to the lake house where he's safe and can heal."

"As soon as the doctors give us the okay, we're out of here. Of course, we'll have to come back for the trial, but until then, it's best to stay clear of Seattle."

"Agreed," Fletch said as they walked out of the thick wooden doors of the study, and for the first time in his life, he didn't cringe.

In fact, after years of dreading setting foot in that place, Fletch felt nothing. No fear, panic, or anxiety.

The place was dead to him now, and it would stay that way.

Chapter Eighteen

One month later

Three o'clock in the morning and Fletch sat watching his brother's chest rise and fall. Elias was asleep on the rollaway bed the nurse had brought in, but Fletch couldn't sleep. Every time he closed his eyes, the nightmares would come, and he'd be back in that desert, turning the sand red with his blood.

The doctors had cleared Kyle to travel now that his most recent surgery was well on the way to healing. Elias was down for the weekend, having returned to work in Marshall after being informed that Fletch's brother's hospital stay would be over a month long with numerous surgeries scheduled. They'd rebuilt Kyle's legs with metal rods, plates, and screws without a guarantee he'd ever walk again.

Fletch didn't begrudge his lover for leaving. Elias was the sheriff. He had responsibilities, and Kyle was safe. They still hadn't been able to track down his father, but the bastard was running out of places to hide. Officers had all ports of entry and exit closed. The highways were patrolled by the local police, and the FBI were involved in the manhunt. Being so close to the Canadian border, he couldn't rule out Charles could've made it to British Columbia before they realized he was missing. They'd checked his passport to no avail, but that didn't mean he didn't have a fake. The RCMP was working in unison with the FBI on that possibility.

The longer it took to find him, the more stress he could feel coming from his brother. The evil man who'd sired them had been responsible for a lot of the physical and emotional abuse Kyle had suffered as they tried to get the location of the safe out of him. The man and woman found in the living room were local thugs hired to keep him hidden.

Charles hadn't informed the cartel there'd been a security breach, knowing he and Elizabeth would be held accountable since it was their son who'd gotten the goods on everyone. They'd planned to get the information out of Kyle and make it, and him, disappear before the powers that be found out. No harm, no foul. Except they hadn't counted on Fletch and his team, or his brother's determination to do what was right.

Kyle's assistant, the man who'd reported him missing, had been found in a dumpster over on Emerson and Thirty-fourth street. The prime suspect in the murder was Detective Roserio, the original officer assigned to the case.

It was refreshing to see Police Chief Roady acting like a dog with a bone. A vicious dog at that. If there was one thing the man couldn't stand, it was dirty police officers and judges. According to the chief, they'd broken their oath to protect the weak and innocent and deserved whatever they got. Fletch definitely liked the guy.

Unfortunately, Kyle had taken full responsibility for his assistant's death. He believed his friend would still be alive if it weren't for his mistake.

That mistake was trusting his parents to do the right thing when Kyle had given them a chance. If he hadn't done that, he would have never gone missing, and his assistant would still be alive. The news had caused a setback in his healing as Kyle's depression worsened.

Fletch didn't know what to do as his brother dove deeper into guilt. No matter what he said, Kyle wouldn't listen, and Fletch was beginning to worry.

"If you keep staring at me, I'm going to get a complex or some shit." Kyle's sleep-roughened voice brought Fletch out of his thoughts.

"We wouldn't want that," Fletch joked, hoping to bring a smile to his brother's face. When he did in fact smile, Fletch felt ten feet tall.

"What time is it?"

"A little past three."

"Why aren't you sleeping?" Kyle asked, looking over at the spare bed. "Your man is here. You should be with him."

"I'll try when I get tired."

"Bullshit. Why aren't you sleeping?" Kyle called him out.

"I have plenty of demons waiting for dreamland," Fletch admitted. "They'll get their piece of flesh eventually."

"Your nightmares have come back?" Kyle asked, looking concerned.

"Do they ever really go away?" Or did they lie in wait?

"I guess not. You should talk to someone about them," Kyle, of all people, said.

"Sure, as soon as you do."

"I'm not ready for that, bro," Kyle said as he shook his head. "I can't relive it now."

Fletch could understand that. "Promise me when you are ready, you'll go. Therapists can truly make a difference. I've seen it with teammates."

"Maybe you should listen to your own advice. As for me, I can't even think about that right now."

"Understood. Let's leave that be for now. How are you feeling?" Fletch asked, hoping for any improvement.

Kyle took a moment to analyze his body. "Not so bad. Now that the infection is gone, I'm beginning to feel much better."

"Good. We'll be heading back to Marshall soon. The doctors have said you're able to travel." Fletch couldn't wait to break his brother out of the hospital and take him home to relax and heal. Julia had been preparing Kyle's new bedroom at the lake house.

Kyle's eyes darkened. "Do you think that's a good idea? They could come looking for me, and Charles is still out there. I could be putting your friends in danger this time."

"Don't worry about us." He grinned. "Ah, we know how to defend ourselves." Kyle shook his head. "All I want you to do is concentrate on healing."

Kyle nodded as he looked away. "I was an idiot," he groaned. "I should've known better."

It was a quick change in subject but Fletch could roll with it. "No. You aren't an idiot. You're a good person and couldn't imagine any of this happening."

"In my mind, I couldn't help but think they were being forced to participate because of Dad's gambling addiction. Instead, they were as dirty as the others. They didn't give a shit about me or those women being trafficked across the country."

"They're sociopaths. They're only concerned about themselves and are willing to destroy anyone for their personal gain. Hell, he even turned on his partner in crime, our mother, and left her for the police to find. Nothing you could've done would've changed that."

"What's going to happen to the women? Will they be sent back to Mexico?" By the tone of Kyle's voice, he wasn't keen on that idea.

"Spence is working on that. We have a couple of ideas, but we haven't received confirmation yet. I'll let you know as soon as we get word."

Kyle smiled and said, "Is there anything your team can't do?"

"I'll let you know when I come across something," Fletch teased.

His brother chuckled, and his eyes began closing. Kyle needed a lot of rest to heal, but he was fighting it.

"Go back to sleep, man. It's early. It'll be hours before sunrise."

"Only if you go lie down with Elias and do the same."

He loved his brother. So much. "Okay, okay." He raised his hands in defeat before standing.

Fletch leaned down and kissed his younger brother on the top of his head. Kyle's eyes were already closed as he walked the few steps over to the rollaway bed. He slipped off his boots, pulled back the covers, and slid in beside his man, who immediately wrapped his arms around Fletch and pulled him close.

"Good night, big brother."

"Good night, Kyle."

***

Elias looked at the clock on the wall for at least the tenth time. Where the hell were they? Fletch, Kyle, and the team were due back over thirty minutes ago. He, Julia, and Roman waited on the porch for their return home, and his excitement was palpable. He hadn't seen Fletch in a week and a half. He needed his man in his arms to feel whole.

During that time, he'd made sure to get the word out that the community were to contact him if anyone saw a stranger in the area. They couldn't be too careful. Along that same line, Frank Edwards was still on the loose, and his disappearance was driving Elias nuts. It'd been months since the incident at Clancy's bar, and there was still no sign of him. They'd searched barns, warehouses, vacant homes, forests, and the lakes across the county, and still nothing.

Someone had to be hiding him, but they didn't know who since they'd cleared his family and friends. Elias wouldn't stop looking until Edwards was found.

Turning his mind back to his man's arrival, he had to hand it to Julia, who'd made up Kyle's room. She'd put him on the ground floor, making it easier for him to get around in his wheelchair and walker. Elias had built a ramp up to the porch so he could enter the lake house through the garden doors. They were wider than the kitchen door and would be easier to manage. In the bathroom, he'd installed handrails near the toilet and had put in a new roll-in shower.

Elias and Julia had tried to prepare as much as they could before Kyle arrived. Once they saw how he navigated in the house, they could change and add things as necessary. Elias hoped Kyle could find some peace here on Fire Lake. Fletch had reported his brother's depression had worsened, and he was past being concerned.

"What is taking them so long?" Julia asked while looking at her watch. "Their welcome home dinner is going to dry out in the oven if they don't get here soon."

"I'm sure it would still be tasty," Roman said, and Elias had to agree. Whenever Julia treated them to her home cooking, there was nothing left behind.

"Thank you, Roman. My mom was an excellent cook."

"Well, the apple didn't fall far from the tree," Elias said. Her fried chicken was second to none. He couldn't help but smile when he noticed Julia's cheeks flush from their compliments.

He remembered smiling wide when he'd locked up Jake, Julia's former boss, for all the illegal shit he'd done. He'd been after the asshole for over a year. Whenever Elias thought he'd had him, Jake's wealthy family bailed him out. Not the last time, though. Maybe they'd grown tired of his shit, or it could have been the police summary when it came to sentencing recommendations.

After finding out he'd tried to force Julia to prostitute herself so he could get in with the owner and buy Brick's property, Elias had been out for blood. This time when Jake's family came sniffing around, he was sure to mention that the news outlets were only an email away. He was done playing nice, and they had their family name to protect.

In the distance, he could hear vehicles heading in their direction. Sure enough, Fletch's and Brick's trucks slowed as they neared the long driveway before pulling in. Julia was jumping with excitement as they went to meet everyone.

Fletch's smiling face greeted him as he went to the driver's side door and pulled his man into his arms the moment he stepped outside. The feel of Fletch's arms holding him tight was exactly what he needed, and by the way Fletch had buried his face into Elias's neck, obviously, he needed comfort as well.

"I'm so happy to be home," Fletch said before raising his lips to Elias's for a kiss. "I missed you."

"I missed you too," Elias said as soon as their lips parted. "How's Kyle today?"

They turned to look at the other side of the vehicle as Shaw lifted Kyle out of the passenger seat before carrying him to the lake house. Elias had noted Shaw was never far away from Kyle, no matter where they were.

"He's exhausted. The trip took a lot out of him."

"Thanks to Julia, his bedroom is ready. She has mad shopping skills, and an eye for comfort. From now on, it's all about rest."

"That's the best news I've heard. Maybe his mood might lift," Fletch said. "Let's go get him settled."

They followed the rest of the team into the house and Fletch froze when he saw the new ramp. "Did you do that?"

"Yeah. I thought it could be useful when your brother wants to come outside under his own steam."

"Thanks," Fletch said before gifting him with the smile Elias had been missing. "It's perfect, just like you."

Elias couldn't help but chuckle. "I'm so far away from perfect it isn't funny."

"Well, you're perfect to me."

"That's all that matters." And it truly was.

Once they stepped into the house, Fletch went to Kyle's bedroom to help his brother. The other team members were busy taking their bags to their rooms while Brick reviewed the pile of mail sitting on his desk.

It would take more than a couple of days for everyone to settle in after being away for two months. It was great seeing the old place coming alive again as the rooms filled.

Great-Aunt Sophia, the original owner and Brick's relative, would be proud to have this group here. Before her death, Elias had become friends with Sophia and she'd left an indelible mark on him, as had been the case for many folks in the area. Her spirit and empathy touched more people than she knew.

"Elias, will you give me a hand getting dinner on the table?" Roman asked as he and Julia zigzagged around the kitchen.

"On my way," he said, and in this moment, all was good and right in the world.

Chapter Nineteen

Fletch wrapped his towel around his waist and walked out of the hallway bathroom. He'd stood under the hot stream of water, hoping to loosen the tight muscles along the back of his neck. It hadn't worked.

The stress had been building for over two months, and it would take the same amount of time or longer to calm back down. Shaw had declared he'd be staying downstairs to help Kyle, so tonight Fletch would be sleeping in his own bed after being gone for too long. He'd been looking forward to it.

The hallway was dark. The only light coming from the moon through the lone window at the end of the hall. The old lake house was built when people had different expectations for their homes. There was no en suite bathrooms, lofty open spaces, or un-wallpapered walls. They were working on a plan to update the house without ripping out the character and charm that made it special. It was going to take a while 'cause it had to be done right.

He walked into his room and shut the door. Elias was in bed waiting for him. The handsome sheriff was sitting up, leaning against the headboard, reading something on his tablet.

They'd decided to stay together at the lake house for now. He needed to be near his brother to help him rebuild his life, and the house felt like home. Fletch was sure Elias had a nice place in town, but living there held no appeal.

"Anything interesting?" Fletch asked as he removed his towel and laid it over the back of a chair to dry.

When Elias looked up, he set his tablet on the side table and said, "There's nothing as interesting as you are."

Fletch couldn't help but smile. When he went to turn his head to the side, he hissed in pain at his sore muscles and raised his hand to rub the back of his neck.

"Your neck still hurting you?" Elias asked, his eyes narrowed as if he could see through Fletch's skin to the sore muscles below.

"Yeah, from stress. The muscles in my neck feel like concrete, and the shower wasn't helpful." It sucked, but he could take it.

"Come here. Let me have a look."

Fletch crawled into bed beside Elias and turned his back to him. His lover's touch felt good for all of two seconds before he began squeezing the tight, screaming muscles. The pain was instantaneous, and he pulled away. "What the hell? I thought you wanted to help."

"Get back here. I do want to help. It's going to hurt before it feels better."

"I don't think so," Fletch snapped, knowing Elias was right, but he'd never say so.

"Okay. How about this. If you let me work on those muscles, you get to have me do anything you want after I'm done."

"Anything?" Now *this* had possibilities.

"Anything."

Fletch grinned. "Deal." His mind raced with images that would never make it to the silver screen.

"Okay, now get back here," Elias ordered.

"Fine," Fletch agreed before crawling back in beside him.

"I'll use the lube to make rubbing my fingers slide against your skin."

"Well, that's one place I never thought to use it," Fletch teased as he turned around and moved his hair away from his neck.

It wasn't long before those hands of steel were back at it, and he was struggling to keep his groans and grunts to a minimum. He stretched his head forward to give Elias more room to work and dug his fingers into the mattress. Sure enough, after ten minutes, he could feel the knots starting to loosen.

"There you go," Elias crooned as his strong hands worked their magic. "It'll take a couple of days to work them out. Kyle's not the only one in need of peace."

Fletch lowered his chin to his chest and soaked up the care being administered. He'd never had someone to watch over him like this. This was the way you loved someone. His parents weren't the best examples, and the rest of his life had been spent in the service where it was his duty to protect others. Having what Elias offered was a gift Fletch never contemplated.

Looking back on his past relationships, he couldn't remember ever being taken care of. Even when he was sick, he couldn't picture anyone making him soup and bringing him a tissue. For sure, it never crossed his parents' minds.

"Why do you like taking care of me?" The question was out of his mouth before he had a chance to stop it.

"Because I love you," Elias stated like it was a foregone conclusion.

"It's that simple?"

"It is to me."

Fletch leaned back against Elias's chest, needing to be closer to his man, who adjusted his position until his arms were around Fletch's abdomen.

"It's new to me. I've lived so long without it. Don't get me wrong, the team is my family, and they care about me, but this is different," Fletch tried to explain. "I don't know if I'm saying this right." He wasn't a big talker normally, and "emoting"? Ah, no.

"I understand what you're trying to say. I'm a firm believer if you love someone, you show them any way possible. It doesn't make me less of a man to show my emotions," Elias said, confidence threading through his tone.

"My neck is feeling a bit looser, thank you."

"Good. I'll rub the muscles again in the morning before I go to work," Elias said. "Now on to my part of the deal. Have you thought about what you want me to do?"

Fletch had thought about it. How could he not? It wasn't like he got that kind of offer every day. Anything he wanted, but what did he want most? What would make him the happiest? Then it came to him.

"I have, and it requires you to lie flat on your back on the mattress," he instructed.

"Flat on the bed?"

"Yep, and you can't move a muscle. No touching, holding, or moving at any time."

Elias looked at him with a grin. "This isn't what I expected, but I'm game."

Fletch stood, giving his love room to spread out across the queen-size bed. He was a tall man, and his feet hung off the end.

"Raise your hands above your head and leave them there," Fletch ordered. "I want to see what's mine."

Fire flared in Elias's eyes. "All yours as you are to me."

"Completely," he said before moving to the end of the bed. "Now, remember, you can't move."

He climbed onto the bed between Elias's opened legs and ran his hands up from his feet to his thighs, which elicited a moan from his lover. Fletch stopped short of taking hold of Elias's cock and balls, even though he wanted to. Instead, he kept crawling over top of the magnificent body beneath him, stopping for a quick lick to the head of Elias's hard cock before carrying on up until they were face-to-face.

"Now that you've got me where you want me, what are you going to do with me?"

Fletch dove in for a deep kiss filled with the promise of more to come before moving on to tracing Elias's stubbled jaw with his tongue. "I'm going to show you how much I love you."

Over the next hour, Fletch did exactly that. With every kiss, lick, suck, and nibble, he showered his love and attention on the man beneath him who remarkably filled all the empty spaces in his heart.

He'd never feel lonely again.

Chapter Twenty

Elias walked out of his office to meet the new arrivals who'd been seen around town asking about Fletch and Kyle. As requested, business owners had reported them to the sheriff's office right away. Marie had already given him the rundown before he'd come out to meet them.

They claimed to be Fletch and Kyle's sisters and were here to find them after learning about what happened in Seattle. That statement alone had Elias doubting their true intent. Kyle had been in the hospital for over a month, and not once did Lisa and Tanya visit him or show any concern whatsoever.

He'd called Fletch to let him know that his sisters were here, and he was on his way into town to deal with them. In the meantime, he'd be happy to play along with the *distraught* sisters.

He walked past Marie's desk and straight up to the silent women. One was blonde and looked like her father, and the other a brunette who favored her mother. Seeing their coloring, Elias wondered where Fletch had gotten his red hair. No one else in the family had red hair, but it was a recessive gene and could've come from any ancestor.

"Hello, I'm Sheriff Cooper," he said. "How may I help you?"

The moment he held out his hand, he knew neither was going to shake it. That wouldn't do. He moved closer until he stood only a foot away, hand still out, smile plastered on his face. He could tell they were trying to think of some way out of it, but there was none.

With barely any pressure, each took his offered hand and gave it a single shake. Bigoted behavior was a power play. If they wanted him to feel uncomfortable, he'd be sure to give it back to them in spades.

"We're here to claim our brother," Lisa, the dark-haired sister, said. "Please tell us where to find Kyle Daniels."

"Well, straight to the point, I can respect that. However, last I checked, he's not a lost pet but a grown man." Before they could speak, he continued. "I'm sure we can work this out. Please follow me."

He didn't bother waiting to see if they'd follow him. He turned and winked at Marie. "Please get in touch with Deputy Bryant and have her come in." Then he carried on into the conference room. Once they were seated, he closed the door, and the sisters began their spiel.

"Kyle needs help after what he's been through. He needs to return to Seattle where we can care for him," Tanya said, laying on the concern thick. "I hate to think what he has to endure."

It was apparent neither had any emotional ties to their brother, and they didn't seem overly concerned about what their parents were into. "I believe his brother Fletch is taking of him."

The disdain was instant. Their noses scrunched as if they'd smelled something rotten.

"Fletcher can barely get by in this world as it is. He can't take care of our brother properly," Lisa said while waving her hand as if shooing away a fly.

"My understanding is he's a Navy SEAL. From what I know, those guys can take care of anyone and anything."

"More like a grunt used as a human shield for the important people," Tanya huffed in a way that left no doubt about what they thought of Fletch's service to his country and the worth of the people he'd saved.

"Has Kyle reached out to you?" he asked. He was enjoying seeing how far these two would go.

"No, but he probably hasn't been given a chance," Lisa said. "You don't understand. Kyle isn't safe with Fletcher."

"Not safe? Wasn't he the one who saved Kyle?"

The women looked at each other, deciding on a different tactic because this one was going down in flames. He waited patiently, knowing Fletch would soon be here.

"He's after our brother's money. Kyle is worth millions and Fletch is trying to cash in on this moment."

"Moment. You mean when your parents kidnapped your brother and severely beat him because he had proof they were trafficking women from Mexico?" he asked.

"Listen, don't believe everything you hear," Tanya advised. "Kyle is a troubled man."

"So now it's Kyle who has the mental problems and not Fletch?" He could go on all day. He was having too much fun with this.

"Fletcher has been a stain on our family since the beginning, and he'll use Kyle for everything he's got. We have to save him."

The conference room door flew open. "Kyle has been saved from our fucked-up family. You have no business here," Fletch announced as he stormed in, catching his sisters off guard. "Where were you when he was missing? Or hell, even in the hospital? Care about Kyle, bullshit. Who sent you here?" Fletch demanded.

Elias had been wondering that as well. The sisters coming out of the woodwork like this hadn't been expected. Certainly not after being MIA during the kidnapping and afterward when Kyle was hospitalized. Elias's guess: they wanted control over Kyle's millions. There was no real concern for their brother's welfare or condition, considering neither had even asked how the man was feeling.

Both women jumped up from their seats, and Lisa's lip turned in a snarl as she snapped, "What the hell are you doing here?"

"You're the one keeping Kyle from us," Tanya yelled before turning to Elias. "What is he doing here?" Elias shrugged and continued smiling.

"Keeping Kyle from you? Neither one of you gave a shit when he was missing or lying in that hospital bed. You two care only about yourselves, the same as our parents."

"We have a legal right to see our brother," Lisa demanded. Elias wasn't going to tell them they had no rights to see Kyle. He was a grown man in control of his mental faculties who could decide who saw him when and where. But he hoped they wasted their time and money on trying.

Fletch pulled out his phone and opened a video. Kyle was lying in his bed back at the lake house, appearing upset, which angered Elias.

"I don't want to see my sisters, and I don't want to leave my brother Fletcher." Then he turned to someone off-screen. "You won't let them take me away."

A voice Elias knew was Shaw's reassured him. "I'll never let them take you. I swear it."

Fletch turned off the video. "Kyle wants nothing to do with either of you. I can't blame him after you ghosted him in his time of need."

"There you have it, ladies, video proof Kyle Daniels does not want to see either of you," Elias concluded before standing, and then moving to the door. "Now if you don't mind."

"He's being forced to say those things," Lisa declared.

"They're brainwashing him," Tanya yelled. "Who was the other man talking in the video?"

"His nurse," Fletch said, and Elias had to agree. Shaw hadn't left Kyle's side for long, and all the SEALs had some level of training to attend to field dressings and more.

"You have him hopped on drugs, don't you? You've always been the stain we could never erase from the family," Lisa attacked.

Fletch, god love him, smiled wide. "That is one thing we can agree on, sis. Neither of us wanting me to be a branch on this parasite-ridden family tree."

Both looked like they'd been slapped, and Elias took the opportunity to insert himself between them and his man. "As sheriff of this county, I find no reason for either of you to be concerned about Kyle's welfare. I have a deputy waiting to escort you to the edge of my county because I don't believe you will leave willingly. Also, heed my warning. If you choose to come back and cause these fine residents I'm entrusted to protect any aggravation, I'll be forced to arrest both of you."

"What the hell?" Lisa shouted. "You can't stop us." Both sneered at him.

Elias puffed out his chest and said, "You may not respect me as a person, but you will respect this badge." He pointed at the metal star over his heart. This time he didn't bother being polite and herded them out the door and into the reception area as they continued to argue.

Deputy Bryant came over to lead the sisters out the door because the last thing he wanted Fletch to do was get involved.

"Either you both calm down, or you'll be spending the night in a cell for disturbing the peace," Elias warned, which sobered both women up quick and they took a step back. "Now that I have your attention, Deputy Bryant here will follow you to the county line.

Don't come back. Kyle has made his decision, and he wishes to stay where he is."

"You'll be hearing from our lawyer," Tanya threatened. "You'll never get away with this."

"With what money?" Spence's voice rang out. "Or were you referring to your parents' lawyer, who's a little tied up at the moment as he's sitting in a jail cell since he's their accomplice?"

Elias turned to see Spence sitting behind the reception desk beside Marie. His laptop was open, never a good sign if you're the person who pissed him off. He looked over at Fletch, who was standing in the doorway. Fletch shrugged and wore an expression that said *carry on*.

"What do you mean 'what money'?" Elias asked. What the hell else could be going on in this family?

"Seems the lovely ladies are penniless, much like their parents." Spence didn't even bother to look up from his screen.

"That's a lie," Tanya spat.

"Nope, your bank accounts are almost empty," Spence said calmly. "I would know. You both have barely enough to pay your mortgage, which is coming due in a few days. Odd, both of your paychecks have stopped being deposited. Perhaps the boss wasn't so sure about having the daughters of the FBI's most wanted in their labs or on their payroll."

The sisters looked at each other and Elias couldn't help but say, "Not what you expected when you came here today, is it?"

"Neither of you are married and you live together," Spence continued. "Shocking."

Fletch laughed, and Elias wanted to join in, but he remained professional. That couldn't be said for Marie, whose deep laughter echoed through the building.

"Your bank accounts were drained six weeks ago. Ironically on the same day your father took off on the run from police."

"What the hell? Did he ask you for money to get away?" Fletch asked, his face a mask of anger. "What is wrong with you two?"

Tanya opened her mouth to answer, but Lisa grabbed her arm and dragged her out the front door. "This isn't over," she yelled over her shoulder.

Deputy Bryant followed them out, shaking her head. "This day is looking up."

"Do you think they gave the psycho the money to get away?" Elias asked. That shit was messed up. Even if they didn't know their father had beaten Kyle to within an inch of his life, they had to know their father was a criminal when he showed up at their door demanding money to evade the police while their mother was left holding the bag. Nope. You couldn't get more fucked up than that.

"I wouldn't put it past them," Fletch said.

"Was it a family or a cult?" Elias asked. Blindly following their father, whose gambling was the catalyst to all of this, indicated all sorts of family weirdness.

"Somedays, I wonder that myself," Fletch answered as Elias squeezed his shoulder.

Marie came over to stand with them. "So, they thought they could come here, make up some story, and the local yokels would hand over that poor man to them?"

"I guess in a way they did," Elias answered. How deluded and entitled could they be?

"You bet they did," Fletch answered. "They'll be back."

"We'll be ready for them," Elias assured.

"We should report our suspicions to Detective Ray," Spence said. "Their financials make for interesting reading, that's for sure."

"I'll give him a call and let him know what happened," Elias agreed. "I don't know how dirty they are, but something is off, and we need to know what that is."

"Thanks," Fletch said. "To all of you for helping my brother stay safe."

Marie came closer, took hold of Fletch's hand, and said with grandmotherly affection, "Don't worry. I can still shoot straight. They come snooping around here, they might get a case of buckshot in their skinny asses."

Fletch's mouth fell open, and Elias laughed.

Chapter Twenty-One

Fletch emerged from the forest to find his brother sitting on the porch in his wheelchair staring out at the lake. Shaw was by his side, and Fletch was beginning to wonder if more was going on there. His brother had never told him he was gay, and to the best of Fletch's knowledge, Kyle hadn't had any gay lovers. Now wasn't the time to ask, but that day would come. His brother wasn't going to be another notch on Shaw's belt.

Even though Shaw was family, Fletch couldn't deny his friend's track record. "Love 'em and leave 'em" had been his MO for as long as Fletch had known Shaw.

Earlier, he'd had to go and reset one of their forest sensors about a quarter of a mile away near the water's edge. It kept going off. They still hadn't found what was triggering it, and considering they never found anyone when they searched, he was beginning to think it was an animal.

There'd been no sister sightings since they'd left, and he figured it could have something to do with the current investigation into their lives. Ray had run with the information Elias had given him, and the sisters had been answering a lot of pointed questions ever since.

There'd still been no word on where their father was hiding, and at times Fletch wondered if the cartel had caught up with him. The trafficking had been exposed, the house in Ensenada was under the Mexican police's control, and from what he'd heard, as expected, his mother was rolling over on all of them to get a lighter sentence.

Life was carrying on, and Kyle was smiling more week after week, but PT wasn't going well, frustrating his brother, making his mood swings legendary around the house. The team understood PTSD well and was there to support him even when Kyle's behavior turned angry and he lashed out at whoever was near.

He'd been dealt a crappy hand.

Not only had Kyle discovered his parents' illegal activity, but the lengths they would go to keep their secret. Before that, Kyle had been under the impression they loved him as their son. Fletch figured he'd had it easier since right from the start he knew his parents didn't love him. He wasn't disappointed when they did crappy things. He was positive Kyle never expected them to turn on him. Betrayal was a sharp pill to swallow.

As for the real estate agent Salvador, he claimed Charles had approached him about finding a buyer for the house in Mexico. When he placed the house for sale, he was approached by a representative for the cartel with their human trafficking plan, and Fletch's parents jumped at the opportunity, not giving a shit about innocent women or getting caught. Charles's debt was cleared, and in return he went on with his life. The cartel owned the house even if it wasn't on paper. None of what Fletch learned surprised him.

"Hey, bro, whatcha doing?" Fletch asked as he neared Kyle and Shaw. "Getting some sun."

Kyle's smile was genuine, one of his better days. "I was thinking about going out for a boat ride."

"A boat ride sounds like fun. When do you want to go?" Fletch asked.

"Today looks nice."

Kyle was right. The sun was shining, and the water was so calm the lake was a mirror reflecting the bright blue sky. He looked over at Shaw.

"Of course, I'm coming along." Shaw smiled when Kyle turned to look at him.

"It'll probably take both of you to get me in that boat. Shit. I hate being a problem."

"No problem at all, bro. Let me get everything ready, and we'll take a cruise around the lake," Fletch said before standing.

"Can I come with you while Shaw gets my jacket?" Kyle asked.

"Sure," Fletch said as he came around behind his brother's wheelchair and pushed him down onto the dock.

If this made his brother happy, he'd do it. Hell, he'd do anything if it made Kyle happy. His boat wasn't anything special, but it was miles better than Brick's old metal wreck he used to go fishing. At least his had seats instead of a bucket to sit on.

He locked the brakes on his brother's wheelchair, went onto the boat, and moved a couple of cushions from the front to the back seats for added padding to protect Kyle from the bouncing. Fletch wouldn't drive fast, keeping the vibrations to a minimum.

"I'm guessing you have a few questions about me and Shaw," Kyle said.

Fletch hadn't thought to bring it up yet, but obviously Kyle wanted to talk about it so Fletch asked the obvious, "You're gay?"

Kyle's face darkened. "Yeah, and I know I should've told you, but I was afraid."

"Afraid of me?"

Kyle shook his head. "No, not you. Never you. Of them. I figured if I stayed firmly in the closet our parents wouldn't have a reason to turn on me too. I know I should've stood up like you did, but I don't have the fight in me you do. I didn't think I could take the shit they dealt out and survive it."

Fletch almost laughed. He'd seethed when he was young. Hated what was done to him until rage built up inside him from the abuse he'd suffered. Being a SEAL taught him how to channel the rage into "fight." He sure as hell wasn't born with it. "Don't apologize for engaging in self-protection. I get why you kept yourself to yourself. Had our roles been reversed, I would've done the same thing, bro." Kyle dropped his chin to his chest and looked like he was folding in on himself. Fletch could feel his brother's pain. Their fuckin' parents. Totally insane. "You know, you're one of the bravest people I know. What you did to help those women was amazing and dangerous. Not many people would've done the same. We know the cards we were dealt and did what we had to do to survive. There's no fault or blame in that."

"See." Kyle pointed at Fletch. "Always the hero."

"Yeah, right." Fletch chuckled and was relieved to see Kyle smile.

Roman came running from the house with an armful of blankets. "Here, take these. You might need them," he said as he neared the boat. "You never know when the weather might change."

Fletch looked up. At one time, he'd wanted to tear Roman limb from limb after the Julia fiasco. Now he was a brother to him and part of the team.

"Thanks, man. I appreciate you always thinking of our welfare."

Roman smiled wide. "That's what family does for each other."

"Yeah, it is." And thanks to the team and Elias, Fletch knew what that felt like.

Over the next several hours, they explored along the shallows of the lake. Fletch decided to stay clear of deep water in case the wind and waves picked up. The last thing he wanted was his brother bouncing around.

Kyle's blue eyes seemed to light up the more they explored. Though he didn't talk much, he didn't have to. Fletch knew his brother was enjoying himself, and he made sure to point out every blue heron, egret, and sandhill crane he saw.

This boat ride was the first time Kyle had been any distance from the lake house, and it was good to see him want to venture out. Fletch would take his brother anywhere he wanted to go.

He hoped this new turn would continue, but was aware there'd be setbacks along the way. In this moment, his brother was happy, and that was all that mattered.

***

"What the hell, you're folding?" Spence asked as Shaw threw in his cards. "How am I going to win my money back if you keep folding?"

"A smart man knows when to hold 'em and when to fold 'em," Shaw stated while running his fingers over his sizeable stacks of nickels.

"If you break out in a country song, I'm going to snap your arm in two," Spence threatened, making the entire table laugh.

"These games get heated," Kyle said from his spot between Fletch and Shaw.

"Wait a bit longer, and you might see someone cry," Shaw said while wiggling his eyebrows, making Kyle laugh.

His brother had been coming along these past few weeks and joining in with the team's leisure activities more often. Fletch was happy to see it. The last thing he wanted was for Kyle to stay locked up in his room.

Elias had called to say he'd be late for dinner. He was finishing a couple of reports. They'd saved him a steak with all the fixings and put it in the microwave to keep warm until he got back to the lake house. Elias had moved a lot of his personal items into Fletch's upstairs bedroom, making him feel more settled. Fletch wanted Elias's belongings there mixing with his. Like it should be.

Everything had been calm in their world as the case continued on in Seattle. It felt like a world away, and they worked hard to keep it out of their everyday lives for Kyle's sake. However, the team had yet to take on a new job since they'd returned. The calls were piling up, and they were getting antsy. Not to mention, money was going out, but none was coming in. Fletch didn't relish leaving his brother to go out on a mission, and neither did anyone else, but soon they'd have to.

The telltale squealing of a sensor caught them by surprise, and when Spence looked at his screen, he huffed in frustration.

"It's that one by the water on the south end of the forest again."

"Damn, every time I think that bastard is fixed, it goes off," Fletch huffed and stood. "I'll be right back. Kyle can play for me."

"With your nickels?" Kyle asked.

"Of course, what's mine is yours, bro."

A look came over his brother's face as he picked up the cards. "Don't worry. I got this." Fletch couldn't help but grin as his brother eyed up the competition. "Who's still in?"

"Good luck, guys," Fletch said to his teammates before heading for the door.

The last thing he heard was Brick asking if Kyle was a ringer. They had no idea his brother loved poker and had taught Fletch many years ago.

He grabbed a new sensor from the storage room and soon walked off the porch and into the forest. Dusk had settled in, and it'd be dark before he got back, but he didn't mind. He'd worked in complete darkness so many times as part of his SEAL team that doing it was second nature.

He loved the smell of the forest as night began to fall. Cicadas were silenced while crickets carried on with their nightly song. After having the hot Texas sun bearing down on the vegetation all day, the night brought it back to life. Creatures big and small came out to hunt, and, as always, he brought his gun along, holstered on his hip.

He never knew when he'd come face-to-face with a bear, cougar, or coyote out here. He didn't want to shoot one. This was their habitat, and he preferred to give the animals their space, but if it was a matter of life and death…he'd do what he had to.

As he walked, he thought about how far Kyle had come in the last month. In the beginning, his brother had barely left his room, choosing to remain hidden away. Slowly, he began leaving his door open so he could hear the people in the living room or kitchen.

Day by day, he'd roll his chair farther out of his room until one day he decided to join Fletch, Elias, and Shaw in the living room to watch a movie. Fletch knew his brother loved action movies, the more explosions, the better, and had turned up the volume to entice him to come out.

That was the night that changed everything. From then on, he'd come out of his room multiple times a day and join in discussions from time to time. All the signs were pointing to Kyle rejoining the world physically, but mentally was another thing altogether.

He refused to talk about what their parents had done, and never brought them up. Clearly, he was mentally distancing himself from them to protect himself from what they'd done. As if by not mentioning it, it would go away. That worried Fletch more than Kyle's legs healing. That psychological shit will eat away at a man until there's nothing left of the person he used to be.

Fletch drew in a deep breath, filling his lungs with the cooler evening air before releasing it slowly to lower his stress. He had to remain strong for Kyle no matter how long it took for him to heal.

He was getting closer to the sensor and could hear the water slapping against the shore. The lake was angry today with one- to two-foot swells. The weather was changing, and a storm was moving in. As if to prove him right, Fletch heard and felt the first few raindrops falling and picked up his pace. The last thing he wanted to do was get caught out here when it started pouring.

One hundred yards away from his destination he realized his mistake when he felt the other person's presence. It had been a trap.

"I have you where I want you," a deep voice growled as the skies opened. "Drop your gun to the ground."

Shit.

***

Elias had dried off and changed out of his wet clothing, but Fletch still wasn't back from repairing the sensor. As expected, Elias had been late for dinner and found the rest of the team playing poker when he'd arrived. He'd thought about heating his dinner but decided to wait for Fletch to return.

He looked out at the forest as the rain continued its deluge. "How long has he been gone?" His gut was telling him something was off.

Spence looked up from his hand to the clock on the wall. "A while now. Too long."

"I was thinking the same thing," Shaw said before lowering his cards to the table.

"Let's go find him," Brick said as he walked over to the locked cabinet and slipped the key in. Each grabbed a weapon while Shaw rolled Kyle back into his room.

"Please find him," Kyle said. The fear in his eyes gutted Elias, and he would've done anything to make Kyle feel better, but something was wrong and Elias wouldn't bullshit Fletch's brother, so he nodded and headed for the garden doors.

His man was out there somewhere, and he'd be damned if he came back without him.

Chapter Twenty-Two

"Never thought you'd be stupid enough to come here," Fletch growled as he took in his father's appearance. Track pants and a t-shirt seemed odd on him, and his hair was longer than he usually wore it. "Looking a little shaggy, old man. Guess it's hard to get a decent haircut when you're on the run."

Charles's face twisted in anger. "You think you've won, but I'm the one in control here." He waved his handgun in the air as Fletch eyed his own gun, lying in the mud a few feet away.

"It's always been about control with you," he said to the man who'd been responsible for years of self-loathing and suffering. "You're nothing. You never were. You'll never get near Kyle again."

"It's not Kyle I'm here for, you simpleton." Charles laughed, sounding as if he were a few bricks short of a full load. "That's what's wrong with you. You never could see the big picture." He waved his gun in an arch when he said those words.

"Big picture? How is aiding in the slavery of th0se poor Mexican women and girls, or what you did to your son, part of that picture, you sick bastard?" Fletch was furious. After everything they'd gone through, their delusional father acted as if it were a minor setback in the grand scheme of things.

When he was young, the venom in his father's eyes would've had Fletch writhing on the ground in pain, but now Fletch laughed it off. "Your looks no longer have any effect on me, Chuck."

To anyone watching this scene unfold, they'd think Fletch had lost his damn mind arguing with the man holding the gun, but it was part of his plan. His father couldn't pass up the opportunity to demoralize him at every turn and brag about himself. By dragging their discussion out, he was stalling, knowing the team would find him. They had to've noticed his absence, and they wouldn't wait to do something about it.

"You were always the weakest link in our family. I'd never expect you to understand. It's about money and power. Who has it and who doesn't. I'd be damned if I'd allowed anyone to tarnish my reputation. Once this *ugliness* is over, things can get back to normal."

"Back to normal? You're insane if you believe that's going to happen. Your gambling caused all of this. Your inability to control yourself is the basis for everything bad that's happened in all our lives. It's on you. Besides, you have a new reputation now. You'll never be a free man again. Every day someone will be telling you what to do and when to do it. Then after decades of it, you'll die penniless and alone behind bars."

"They cheated me and charged me insane interest so I could never pay off what I owed." Spit flew from his father's mouth as he raged. "They started this ball rolling. I was protecting myself."

"It's always someone else's fault with you, isn't it? A man takes responsibility for his actions. Not that you taught me that. On top of all your criminal activity, you abandoned your wife to the police while you ran away like the coward I always knew you were."

"There was no use trying to teach you anything. You were a disappointment from the start."

While his father carried on with his tirade, Fletch loaded the toe of his boot with as much sticky, black mud and twigs as possible and waited for his moment. He watched the gun being waved through the air with every word Charles spoke, and when he was pointing it in the opposite direction, Fletch kicked the mud up into his father's face and chest before taking off in the opposite direction of the lake house. He refused to lead him anywhere near Kyle.

His father's shouts were drowned out by the pouring rain and Fletch's pounding heart. He moved through the forest with speed and agility while Charles crashed around like a bear with a mouthful of bees. There was nothing stealthy about the old man.

The first shot ricocheted off a tree to his right, and he picked up the pace. Charles had resorted to firing aimlessly, and for a moment, Fletch thought he was far enough away to avoid being hit. Until he wasn't.

The burning pain raced through his left arm, close to where he'd been shot only a few weeks ago. The impact knocked him off balance and he landed several feet away and headfirst into a tree trunk.

The impact rattled his head, causing his vision to blur when he tried to stand. By the time he recovered enough from the blow to the head, it was too late.

"Thought you could get away from me," Charles gasped as he stormed over a small bush while raising his gun and pointing it at Fletch's head.

This was it. "You'll never leave here alive, old man."

With a smile completely lacking sanity, Charles aimed and said, "Neither will you."

Fletch closed his eyes and pictured Elias. His last few moments would be happy even though they hadn't had a chance at a lifetime. He'd been loved by the best. He heard the gunshot go off, but there was no impact to his body. He opened his eyes to find his father lying on the ground with a bullet wound to the side of his head.

He looked up, expecting to find a teammate, but was shocked when he discovered Frank Edwards standing at least twenty feet away with that big-ass gun of his. Holy shit, talk about going from the frying pan into the fire. Then Frank dropped his gun to the ground.

Moments later, the forest exploded around them as Elias and the team broke through the trees. Elias headed straight for him while the team secured the area.

"Shit, you've been shot again." His man growled as he took in the damage. "And there's a gash on your head. An ambulance is on its way," he said as he pulled off his t-shirt and pressed it against Fletch's bullet wound.

"My father?" he asked.

"Dead." Elias's tone was flat.

Fletch wasn't sure what to say, but the relief was undeniable. He turned to find Frank Edwards with his hands zip-tied behind his back, his head bowed.

"Frank saved me." It felt odd saying those words. "Why, and what's he doing here, I don't know."

The man who'd shot him months ago for being gay had shot Charles before Charles could kill Fletch. He was in too much pain to think on that messed-up chain of events.

"Is Kyle safe?" That was the most important part.

"Yeah. Shaw is protecting him."

"Good, because I think I'm going to pass out." His head swam, his vision darkened, and his legs gave out. Luckily, Elias caught him before he landed back in the mud.

He'd had enough crazy shit happen to him for one day. It was time to reset.

***

Elias hated waiting rooms. Especially the ones in hospitals. This was the second time he'd had to sit out here while the man he loved got stitched up. It was a trend he wanted to end, but he knew that was impossible considering who Fletch was and what he did for a living.

"This is all my fault," Spence said from the far corner of the room, breaking the silence.

"How's that?" Brick asked as he turned to look at Spence.

"I kept sending him out there to replace that sensor. I should've known better. I got lazy." Spence muttered that last bit under his breath.

"What happened to Fletch is Charles Daniels's fault, not yours," Elias said, trying to reassure Spence.

"I should've moved the sensor to another location when I realized something wasn't right," Spence said. "It's because of my mistake Fletch was out there. He could've been killed."

Before anyone could respond, the doctor came out of the swinging doors. "Fletch Daniels's family."

Elias, Brick, and Spence stood.

"How is he?" Elias asked.

"We've removed the bullet from his arm and stitched up the wound. It should heal without any lasting effects. His concussion is another matter. The blow to his head caused swelling of the tissue in that area of his brain."

Elias braced his hand against the wall as a wave of nausea nearly had him chucking up his coffee. Brain injury? "How bad is it?"

"We're monitoring him closely in case there's a chance we have to go in to relieve the pressure. It could still clear up on its own over the next few days. Only time will tell."

"Can I see him?" Elias asked.

"I can allow one of you to go in and see him for a few minutes. He needs to rest."

"You go," Brick said to Elias. "He'll be needing to see you."

Elias nodded. He needed to see Fletch and followed the doctor through the doors. They passed by rows of assessment rooms and into the ICU. "He's in intensive care?"

"It's the best place for him to be monitored in case medical intervention is required." Fuck. A clinical way of saying bad shit could happen.

Machines beeping assailed him as he entered Fletch's room. His man was hooked up to several of them, and his red hair had been shaved to reveal his injury. He looked too pale, and Elias thought the worst until Fletch opened his hazel eyes and smiled.

"Don't scare me like that," Elias huffed as he went to Fletch's bedside and took hold of his hand.

"I have a thick head. There's nothing to worry about," he said.

"How about we leave that up to the doctors?"

"Deal." Fletch smiled again as his eyes drifted closed.

"You get some rest and don't worry about a thing. I've got you."

"I never worry when my big, bad sheriff's around," Fletch mumbled as his eyes closed.

"Love you, Fletch."

He grunted, but it was unintelligible.

Chapter Twenty-Three

The sound of the leaves rustling in the breeze blended with the lapping waves as Fletch stretched out on the lounger set on the porch. It was one of those days that invited you to lie back and enjoy the moment, and that was what he was doing.

It'd been weeks since he'd been released from the hospital, and he was still relegated to the sidelines until his concussion fully healed. The doc had been clear, the next concussion could permanently damage his brain if he hit his head before he was healed from this injury.

Fletch took the warning seriously. A broken bone will heal, but a brain that had been concussed too many times wouldn't. Therefore, here he sat while everyone else prepared for Kyle's surprise. His brother had suffered another setback when he learned of Fletch's injuries. Kyle blamed himself for what happened and returned into his shell. Fletch hoped this surprise helped.

Spence suffered from guilt for sending Fletch out repeatedly to fix the sensor. He was still working on convincing his teammate none of what happened was his fault.

The person to blame was six feet under. It was too easy of an end for a man who'd caused so much suffering in his lifetime. His mother was sitting in a jail cell waiting for her day in court as new arrests continued. Between her assistance and the tapes and other information found in the study, the Seattle PD was busy.

They never heard from his sisters again after they were run out of town, for which everyone was thankful.

As for Frank Edwards, the truth was crazier than fiction. He'd come looking for Fletch, but it wasn't for the reason he'd expected. Frank wanted to turn himself in to Fletch and explain his actions. He'd been a drunk asshole that night and had already decided to back out of the situation when the woman stepped onto the back deck and screamed, jolting him and causing his gun to go off. That night, when he heard the shooting and came across Charles, all his plans flew out the window, and he shot Fletch's father.

Fletch wasn't sure how much of what Edwards said was the truth, but he had to admit Frank dropped his gun the moment Charles was down. Frank hadn't pointed the gun at him at any time and didn't fight back when he was taken into custody. That didn't get him off the hook for his behavior at the bar, but at least he'd proven he wasn't all bad. Most people weren't all good or all bad, except, as luck would have it, his parents. They didn't have a decent bone in their bodies.

Fletch wanted people to stop pointing guns at him. He felt like he was still out in the field where everyone was shooting at him. He'd thought those days were over once he retired. But he had to laugh. He couldn't really think he'd never encounter another situation where guns were involved given the nature of the work LH Investigations did. He couldn't imagine any other life.

He looked down at his watch; it was time for his brother's surprise, and he prayed it didn't go over like a lead balloon. It felt like they were starting back at the beginning, but Fletch couldn't blame Kyle after everything he'd been through. It would take time and therapy to help his brother get his life together, and Fletch would be there to help every step of the way.

After enjoying his last few moments in the sun, he stood and made his way back into the lake house on his way to Kyle's room. He knocked on the door and waited for Kyle to respond before going in. When he answered, Fletch opened the door and saw Kyle lying in his bed watching some game show. He didn't bother to look at Fletch.

"Hey, bro, I got something I want to show you," Fletch said with enthusiasm.

"What is it?" Kyle asked while staring blankly at the TV.

"It's a surprise."

"I don't like surprises anymore."

I bet. "I promise this is a good one."

"Where is it?"

"We have to go on a short drive to get there."

"No, thanks. I'd rather stay here," Kyle stated.

Fletch knelt at the side of the bed and took his brother's hand. "Trust me. I would never do anything to harm you."

"I've heard that before," he quipped.

"Low blow, man. I've done nothing but help you."

Kyle looked away from the game show and turned his sad blue eyes on Fletch. "I'm sorry. I know you have. I can't stop myself from saying stupid things when I'm angry or nervous."

"I understand, bro. You know I do. PTSD is a tough bastard, but you aren't alone." Fletch squeezed his brother's hand in a show of support.

After several minutes, Kyle said, "So, what's this surprise?"

"Will you come with me to see it?"

Kyle sucked in a deep breath and nodded. "Yeah."

Fletch would've given a whoop if he didn't think it would send his brother through the ceiling. Instead, he helped Kyle into his wheelchair and brought him outside and down the ramp to his truck.

"Don't worry. It's safe."

"Will Shaw be there?" Kyle asked.

Fletch didn't allow that question to bother him. He wanted Kyle to have people he could trust and not only him. "Yeah. He's waiting there for us."

Kyle smiled as Fletch lifted him into the passenger seat and buckled him in.

"Ready?"

"As I'll ever be," Kyle said as he seemed to struggle to keep the smile on his face.

"Thanks for trusting me," Fletch said before closing the door, then loading the wheelchair into the bed of the truck, before jumping into the driver's seat.

Without saying another word, he cranked the engine over and backed out of the driveway. Instead of turning toward town, Fletch headed in the opposite direction.

"What's down here?"

"Roman's father owns a place down here, but he's out of the country for a while and he's allowing us to use it." Which surprised Fletch to no end. It was the first decent thing he'd ever known the man to do.

It didn't take long to drive the couple of miles, and soon they were pulling up to the mansion on the hill.

"Nice house," Kyle said as they pulled to a stop and the front doors to the mansion burst open.

The team, Elias, Marie, the deputies, and the fishing crew came out to greet them. Julia and Sammy waved from their spot on one of the balconies, along with a couple of other women he'd met months ago.

"What's going on?" Kyle asked.

Before Fletch could answer, a young woman named Alejandra walked up to the passenger side of the truck and waved.

"What's she doing here?"

"We want to show you what your bravery has done. By saving Alejandra, you set a chain of events into motion, which brings us to today."

Shaw reached for the passenger handle and opened the door. "Hey. I was beginning to miss you."

"Just beginning?" Kyle asked like he was pissed off, making Fletch smile.

Shaw blushed, shocking the hell out of Fletch before saying, "Maybe not just." The always smooth man looked flustered and didn't come back with a witty response.

Fletch jumped out of the truck and lifted Kyle's wheelchair out of the back. Shaw set him down in the chair and took over pushing duties.

Laura and Crystal, the older ladies who'd been caring for the trafficked women, came forward. "Hello, Kyle. I'm so happy to see you again," Crystal said.

"We were so worried," Laura added.

"We're here to celebrate you and what you've done," Crystal stated.

"Me? I didn't do anything. My brother and his team are the people to thank."

Alejandra came forward. "You saved me and took me to a safe place. Without you, none of us would be free." More young women came out of the front door and onto the balcony. "All of us were freed and given a chance at life because of you." The young woman began crying, and she knelt beside Kyle's chair, taking hold of his right hand. "You are my savior."

Kyle's eyes went wide as he looked around at all the smiling faces and then asked, "Will they have to go back to Mexico? There's nothing for them there. How do we stop that?" He was getting worked up.

"They don't have to go anywhere, bro," Fletch said as Elias came over and wrapped his arm around Fletch's shoulder. "We've made sure of it, or, I should say, the miraculous Spence has."

Alejandra wiped her tears away and said, "We are to become American citizens."

"Really?" Kyle asked as he looked over at Spence, who was standing back from the group. "They can stay here?"

"Well, the paperwork is in motion and Roman's father has given us the space we required to house everyone. It'll take time, but yeah, in the end, they'll all be citizens."

"Thanks," Kyle said before looking around at the group. "Thanks all of you. What I did would be worthless if they were forced back into the same situation in Mexico."

Fletch placed his hand on his brother's shoulder. "You did this. You're a hero."

"A hero?" Kyle repeated the phrase, looking a bit stunned.

Alejandra stood and smiled wide. "Come see what we've done to the house," she said while leading Kyle to the front doors as Shaw pushed. "There's so much room here, and I've never seen a kitchen so big. We've cooked a huge meal for all of you."

As the group followed, Fletch and Elias stayed back for a moment. Fletch turned and they were face-to-face.

"Hey there, handsome."

"Hey back," Elias replied, pulling him closer. "It's a good thing you guys did here. I'm proud to be a small part of it."

"You could never be a small part. Without you, I wouldn't't've had the strength to face my family." Elias was the rock by his side who provided him with the courage to face his past.

"I don't know about that, but I do know I love you," Elias said as he dug around in his pocket for something.

"You're ruining the mood," Fletch teased.

"A-ha, got it," Elias mumbled and pulled his hand out of his pocket with his palm closed. "I want you to have this."

When he opened his hand, a gold band appeared shining in the sunlight.

"It belonged to my grandfather, and I want to give it to you because you mean that much to me," he said. "You'll never have to worry about mixed messages again. You are my heart and always will be."

Fletch was struck speechless by the irreplaceable gift. Everything he'd ever wanted in life was his, and so much of it was due to the wonderful man standing in front of him.

He must have taken too long to answer because Elias began talking again. "If you feel it's too soon..."

Fletch pulled him tight and dove in for a kiss full of love and excitement. When he released Elias, he held out his hand.

Elias's eyes were glassy as he slid the ring onto Fletch's shaking finger.

This was the beginning of Fletch's new life on Fire Lake, and he couldn't wait to start it with his sheriff by his side.

ABOUT THE AUTHOR

M. Tasia is a M/M romance author who lives in Ontario, Canada. She's is a dedicated people watcher, lover of romance novels, 80's rock, and happily-ever-afters (once the MCs are put through their paces, of course), who grew up with a love of reading. She's a firm believer that everyone deserves to have love, excitement, and crazy hot romance in their lives. Love should be celebrated and shared.

Connect with M.:
mtasiabooks.com
FB: mtasiabooks
twitter: @mtasiaauthor
IG: @m.tasia.author
TikTok: @mtasiauthor

www.BOROUGHSPUBLISHINGGROUP.com

If you enjoyed this book, please write a review. Our authors appreciate the feedback, and it helps future readers find books they love. We welcome your comments and invite you to send them to info@boroughspublishinggroup.com.

Follow us on Facebook, Twitter and Instagram, and be sure to sign up for our newsletter for surprises and new releases from your favorite authors.

Are you an aspiring writer? Check out www.boroughspublishinggroup.com/submit and see if we can help you make your dreams come true.

Love podcasts? Enjoy ours at www.boroughspublishinggroup.com/podcast